UPON A
ONCE TIME

UPON A ONCE TIME

"Where The Earth Meets The Sea And The Sea Meets The Sky" ©2020 Brent Baldwin
"Mutability" ©2020 Maya Chhabra
"Sunshine Noir For Synthetic Lovers" ©2020 Lin Darrow
"Taketori Momogatari" ©2020 Evan Dicken
"The Pilot" ©2020 CJ Dotson
"Gell Who Makes" ©2020 Kit Falbo
"Abigail Washington And The Angelic Organ Of Far Khitan" ©2020 Joshua Gage
"Currants To The Sea" ©2020 Taryn Haas
"The Forest Magic Protects Its Own" ©2020 Jamie Lackey
"The Rabbi's Daughter And The Golem" ©2020 Alex Langer
"Cloak Of Bearskin" ©2020 Anna Madden
"Two Of Our Kind" ©2020 Anna Martino
"Diamonds, Toads, And… Pumpkins?" ©2020 Melissa Mead
"The Candlewood Trail" ©2020 Dennis Mombauer
"The Waters At The End Of The Worlds" ©2020 Mike Morgan
"Lady Of The Slake" ©2020 Suri Parmar
"Red Boots Blues" ©2020 Cat Rambo
"Strings That Ought To Be Pondered, Even In Urgent Times" ©2020 M. Regan
"A Dark Path Through The Forest of Stars" ©2020 Jude Reid
"Six Rusalki" ©2020 NA Sulway
"Little Tom's Reality" ©2020 Rebecca E. Treasure

*Special thanks to Bob and Kathy Gallagher and Sarah Marshall
for their generous grants.*

All Rights Reserved.
No part of this book may be used or reproduced in any manner whatsoever without written permission, except in the case of brief quotations embodied in critical articles and reviews.

AIR AND NOTHINGNESS PRESS
2224 DELAWARE AVENUE | PITTSBURGH, PENNSYLVANIA 15218
WWW.AANPRESS.COM | INFO@AANPRESS.COM

SECOND EDITION - 2020

aan20.05.2
Printed in the United States of America
ISBN: 978-1-7358356-0-0

SIX RUSALKI NA Sulway	9
THE WATERS AT THE END OF THE WORLDS Mike Morgan	21
LITTLE TOM'S REALITY Rebecca E. Treasure	35
DIAMONDS, TOADS, AND… PUMPKINS? Melissa Mead	47
THE RABBI'S DAUGHTER AND THE GOLEM Alex Langer	59
ABIGAIL WASHINGTON AND THE ANGELIC ORGAN OF FAR KHITAN Joshua Gage	71
STRINGS THAT OUGHT TO BE PONDERED, EVEN IN URGENT TIMES M. Regan	79
LADY OF THE SLAKE Suri Parmar	87
RED BOOTS BLUES Cat Rambo	97
TAKETORI MOMOGATARI Evan Dicken	103
TWO OF OUR KIND Anna Martino	115
CURRANTS TO THE SEA Taryn Haas	125
CLOAK OF BEARSKIN Anna Madden	137
SUNSHINE NOIR FOR SYNTHETIC LOVERS Lin Darrow	145
THE CANDLEWOOD TRAIL Dennis Mombauer	157
GELL WHO MAKES Kit Falbo	167
MUTABILITY Maya Chhabra	179
THE PILOT CJ Dotson	187
A DARK PATH THROUGH THE FOREST OF STARS Jude Reid	199
THE FOREST MAGIC PROTECTS ITS OWN Jamie Lackey	211
WHERE THE EARTH MEETS THE SEA AND THE SEA MEETS THE SKY Brent Baldwin	221

"The way to read a fairy tale
is to throw yourself in."

W.H. Auden

THE PIED PIPER OF HAMELIN • RUSALKA TALES • FANTASY

SIX RUSALKI

NA SULWAY

Every ten years our mother bore a daughter. One after another after another. And though each of us was perfect, with ten fingers and a tail, button noses and sharp teeth, our father was not satisfied. What good were daughters, he railed, when there were wars to fight, alliances to ratify, a kingdom to reign over. Daughters could not lead an army or wield a sword. They could not own property or rule, even as regents. Women's minds were addled as coral. The eggs in our bodies made us weak. If we could not breed we were worse than useless. One daughter in a gam of sons would have been fine: a pretty decoration at state dinners, a marriageable asset. Five was a shame our father could not bear.

Surely, his advisors whispered, our mother was a secret enemy. Five spawnings and no sons? Wasn't she the granddaughter of his father's enemy? Look at how each daughter had his wife's Rusalki hair—not the flowing gold of his own people, the Näkki—and how his wife and daughters spoke to each other in their garbled, impenetrable tongue. What did they say to each other? Why did they bite down on their words when he entered a room? Look at how his wife swam across the oceans each summer to visit her brother. Were his wife and her brother plotting revolution, in that distance tide? Casting spells against our father and his nation? Perhaps we were not his daughters at all, but the daughters of some unnatural passion?

At the end of the sixth decade of their marriage, when our mother came home, she entered a court barbed against her. Her belly swelled but our father looked askance. *Is it a son?* he said. *Is it* my *son?*

When my youngest sister was born, he had our mother executed. And along with her, our uncle and our grandmother. Their heads were mounted on pikes outside our window. We were allowed to swim out and mourn them. To cut away the hair from their heads, as Rusalki women have always done, and divide it among ourselves.

I picked six scales from my mother's throat: one for each sister. In our room, late at night, I showed my sisters how to slip the scale under their tongues and use them to recall our mother: her tenderness and her ferocity, her history and her language. I showed them, too, how to use the scales to send messages to each other, and to me. My second youngest sister, only ten years old, was so little she delighted in her new skill: casting messages to her sisters in the next room about her starfish companion.

What tender mercy stopped our father from having our heads mounted on pikes at the gates of his castle? Our long hair streaming in the tide till it loosed from our bones and tangled with the weeds? There would have been no daughters to collect our memories.

But a father's heart is a father's heart, after all, and while we each had our mother's hair, and our mother's dark eyes, he saw enough of himself in us that his heart was swayed. Still, his alliance with our mother's kingdom was done, and a new bride waited for him: a new alliance. After months of uncertainty and imprisonment, he declared his marriage to the 'foreign woman' had never been legal, and declared her daughters therefore illegitimate. Finally, confident that six illegitimate daughters without any legal claim on either his own throne or that of our dead mother could ever pose a threat, he sent us each into a different exile.

I am my mother's oldest daughter: perhaps that's why my exile was so distant and so deep. I was sent into a well. For many years I granted wishes to the women of a nearby town. All their wishes were the same: love, they wanted. The love of a mother or a man. Or, when their hearts were broken, they asked for revenge. In exchange, they gave me silver needles and bracelets made of hair. The bones of sparrows and the blood of horses. Finally, a woman came who asked me what I wished for.

Freedom, I told her.

She asked me what that was, for a woman, and I said if she wished it, we could find out together.

For fifty years we roamed the northern steppes. One night we were camped by the Black Sea. The stars swarmed over our heads, and the horses were restless in their pen. I took the black hank of my mother's hair from my pack, her scale from my pocket, and went into the water. I washed her hair and combed it, then plaited it in with my own. I placed her scale beneath my tongue and felt her rage—the rage of our mother and our grandmother—rise in my breast. And heard, too, as I had not before, my youngest sister's casting.

It took another ten years for my sisters and I to escape our various exiles and gather in this dry place. All of us but the youngest. We each have our own tent, and our own bath. By day we bathe, our bodies supple in their tanks. At night, we shuck off our seaskins and gather to sing the battle-songs of our mother's and our grandmother's people. The nameless women of the deep. Above us the stars crowd, the moon wanes.

My mother's second daughter was exiled to a lake. She had always preferred stillness, and so the great expanse, its surface like a mirror of the sky, pleased her. She was wont to lie sleeping in its great depths, only occasionally rising to ruffle the surface with her breath. She taught the local women what she knew of magic, and took their husbands' swords as tribute in return. She kept the blades in a deep cave, where the anoxic water soon grew sweet with the taste of steel and iron.

Once, she offered a great queen one of her swords—an enchanted blade named Excalibur—in exchange for our father's head. But the queen's husband stole it, wielded it in his own name, and would not pay the price. When my sister came to his court to claim her reward, ice-water dripping on his marble floors, his knights raised their swords to her throat.

She killed them all and took his crown, and his wife, for her own.

My mother's third daughter was exiled to a river. Each day, she passed beneath seven bridges. The last of the bridges joined a walled city to its fields.

An old man slept beneath the seventh bridge, sometimes gazing into the water, sometimes burning dry moss to warm his hands. His eyes were dark as moonless night, his brow wide and furrowed as a field. His hair was long and tangled, thick with grease. In it, he had woven shells and beads, stones and coins. He slept there, in the cold dark, and muttered in his sleep. Sometimes he trailed his fingers in the water; long threads of bitterness flowed from him.

My sister gave him a pipe, which she had enchanted with the river's voice, and taught him how to use it to charm fish into his net. He was a quick study. Soon enough he knew a song for charming toads into buckets, for emptying a house of rats.

He told her, too late, the source of his bitterness. How a woman he loved had not loved him well enough in return. How he'd only struck that once-was-wife of his twice, maybe three times. How it was not his fault she'd broken so easily. Her bones were brittle as a bird's, he said. But the people of the town had taken her word against his. The bailiff had come and cast him from his own fine house, his own soft bed. And now that once-was-wife kept their brood of children from him: their grubby fists and pink cheeks. Spilled dark tales of him in their ears, he was sure, to sharpen their fear of him.

One night, he came down to the dampness under the bridge with a trail of children in his wake. His own and his neighbours'. The judge's twins, and the children of the bailiff; the oldest carrying the youngest in his arms. He charmed them down to the shore with his pipe, where he summoned my sister and told her to carry them far out to sea, then drown them.

My sister gathered the children in a great boat woven of her hair, and made ready to leave. Before she left, she bid the piper bend down to receive a kiss. Fool that he was, he came and knelt on the riverbank. She took him in her good strong arms. She rolled him in the river until he was cold and still and blue. Buried him beneath a stone where his bones still rattle when the river runs.

Hers is the largest tent: the children's army sleeps within.

Our mother's fourth daughter was exiled to a pond. It was a bounded, pretty thing, with lilies and frogs. Not very deep, not very grand, but comfortable enough. The sun warmed its depths each day, and at night the lightning bugs danced over its surface. One late summer a young boy dropped his golden ball into the pond and my sister retrieved it for him, in exchange for which she was thrown against a wall. Every bone broken. Her lip split and the whites of both eyes turned red with blood.

She didn't kill him. She sang him the song of undoing. His thoughts unravelled. He scratched at his skin, believing something terrible swam in his blood. He opened all the taps in his home and let the rooms flood. Water ran across the floors, into the walls, down the stairs. Everything was soft and rotten and bloomed with mould. Paper peeled from the walls; the books in his library swelled and ran. Chairs floated out of the windows into the street. My sister swam through the downstairs rooms, delighted. Released.

My mother's fifth daughter was exiled to a sideshow. She was kept in a glass tank, shadowed by velvet curtains. The lid of the tank was a heavy brass grille, kept closed with a brass padlock. Only the man who had bought her from our father had a key. Along with my sister the man bought a boy of our kind—green-eyed, gelded—to be my sister's keeper. There was a symmetry to their joint exile: he had been stripped of both his sex and his seaskin, and could no longer become his true Rusalki self. She had had the hair shorn from her head, and could no longer transform into a landwalker.

The keeper called him Boy and made him sleep on a bed of straw. Once a month Boy was allowed to open the grille and clean the glass walls of my sister's tank. He did not have his own key; instead, the owner came into the room, climbed the ladder, turned the lock.

Their owner kept the key at the end of a brass chain soldered to a heavy brass cuff, which was locked around his wrist. Every month, for the first five years of her captivity, my sister rose to the surface of the water to beg him to release her. She held onto the bars of the grille and lifted herself towards him. First she wept, then she wheedled. After five years she lost patience and spat black poison, killing the nerves on one side of his face. Even then, she was too valuable an asset for him to release. He grinned at her, wiped the spit from his cheek with a kerchief.

For six months her tank was not cleaned.

Gentlemen paid a dollar to have the curtain pulled aside and peer into the murk in which she lived. To see a flick of her tail, the blur of her hand against the glass. They were given earplugs to wear, and warned not to remove them. On Sundays she was fished out of the tank and laid on a lounge that soon grew rotten with salt. The velvet frayed and the hessian and springs beneath poked at her skin.

Still, she was strange. And a certain kind of man will pay a great deal to touch something so unusual. Not so gentle men paid upwards of a month's earnings to spend a quarter hour alone in her company. By the end of their time her breathing would be shallow, her eyes glooming dry. She would breathe slowly, hissing a little, through clenched teeth. Her cold skin would grow warm, her scales would start to dry and curl. Her hair would cease its writhing, lay damp and limp across her throat. To keep her alive, Boy would pour buckets of saltwater over her head, dampening the bed and our sister, sending floods of water over the floorboards and her gentleman visitor's shoes.

The gentle men had sharp fingers and blunt desires. They fumbled at her breasts and belly, but could find no soft hollow to penetrate. Her mouth, like my own, is filled with rows of teeth. Twenty rows of placoid scales, sharp as scissors. They were warned against her cloaca, which would sever any organ it enfolded. Boy smirked and said nothing as, one after another, they left her chamber defeated.

She was the hardest to contact: the last to come to our camp. She still had our mother's scale, but she kept it, for many years, on a silver chain around her neck. She could not bear, she said, to know what terrors our father had made for the rest of us. It was Boy who asked her about it; Boy who convinced her that she was strong enough to feel her mother's rage writhe through her winnowed body.

One Sunday, as she lay on that rank lounge enduring the affections of a stranger, she looked up at Boy. His fists were clenched around the handle of his bucket. His jaw was tight. Rusalki men never weep: their bodies are largely formed of water. Water is what they breathe. But after being trapped in the body of a landwalker for so long, Boy's body had changed.

My sister, having lived within it for almost as long as she could remember, could endure her own abasement, her own pain, but she could no longer endure his. The scale hung ready at the end of its chain. All she had to do was slip it under her tongue and lock it into place to feel our grandmother's rage, our mother's rage, the rage of her sisters. To find the strength to raise her arms to the stranger mewling at her breast and pluck out his ear plugs. She sang him to an easy death—just a little blood trickled from his ear—then turned on her keeper.

Boy grinned at my sister as she sang their keeper into the tank, she dragged him down into its murky depths and tethered his body to the rocks in the bottom of the tank, padlocking him

into his own cage. My sister and Boy took the keeper's truck and
drove to the nearest river. She swam one hundred miles upstream
to reach us; he drove alongside, keeping level with her mile by
mile. She is learning to swim in wild water again. Her hair grows
longer every day.

• •

My youngest sister was not sent into exile. She was so young
at the time that our father thought she could do no harm,
and instead betrothed her to the son of a landling king whose
holdings spread from the shore of my father's kingdom to the
great wastes of the north. When she was still a youngling—just
fifty years of age by our reckoning; ten by the reckoning of the
landlings—our father peeled off her seaskin and gave it to the
king as part of her bride-price. She was stripped of her scales
and her gills and her tail, sent to be raised alongside her future
husband: a bonded slave in golden bracelets.

Every dark moon she is let into a room at the top of a great
tower and the door is locked behind her. Inside the room there
is a deep wooden bath. Her seaskin waits for her, folded over
the back of a chair. She knows that her future father-in-law
has worked a hole into the wooden door; that he watches as
she peels off her dress, her bodice, her stockings and shoes. As
she takes her seaskin into the water and turns. Knows, too, that
when she sings, he cannot stay close, cannot peer at her as he
wishes. Her song itches at the inside of his skull. The song of
the whale and the weed and the deep. It is a woman's song, which
no man can tolerate without his blood turning to ash; his heart
seizing in its nest.

Outside the bathing chamber she is silent.

She has not spoken a word since they claimed her.

She may be the future bride of the prince—a valuable token of an alliance with our father's kingdom—but to the landlings we are closer to animals than to gods. They do not trust our father; they do not trust my sister, either, or any of our kind. And they want to know our secrets: what we hold in our ocean halls, how many kingdoms there are, how many soldiers might rise against them if they claim our territories as their own. My youngest sister is a proud and ferocious woman. No matter that the king's persuader pierces her ankles with a hot iron, or drives needles into the soles of her feet. When she leaves his torture rooms, she dances. She smiles at him, pityingly, and dances.

Her feet leave a trail of blood from basement to ballroom.

The morning after the dark moon, our youngest sister is to be wed to her mortal husband. Our father is coming—he will be a guest of honour at the wedding feast—with his retinue of knights. As is the custom at weddings, our father will come unarmed. And the landling king and his son will lock up their swords in the armoury.

We will gather outside the city: the secret our little sister will not speak. Our swords, our arrows, our army of children. Soon, soon, our littlest sister will walk down the aisle between our father's unarmed army and that of the landling king. They are keen to see the alliance made. Keen for the feast and the wine and the dancing. Keen to see the sheet, stained with her virgin blood, hung from the window after her husband beds her. Her blood spilled to seal their treaty.

She will keep her head low as she walks. She will be cloaked in a long veil, trailed by six women with blades concealed in their bouquets. She has tied our mother's hair into her own; our grandmother's locks, too, tangle and writhe down our sister's back. When her husband lifts the veil and leans to kiss her, he will be the first to know, as her teeth tear open his throat, that we have returned.

Our teeth are sharp, and we are ready.

N.A. Sulway's previous publications including short stories, poems and essays in a range of Australian and international publications, as well as six book-length works. Her most recently published books are the adult fiction novel *Dying in the First Person* (Transit Lounge), and a children's novel, *Winter's Tale*.

THE WATERS AT THE END OF THE WORLDS

MIKE MORGAN

For seventeen years the emperor of Wormkind commanded his legions to search for the waters of eternal life. Desperate to prolong his existence, he sent agents to worlds beyond measure, scouring every reality for the faintest trace of his hoped-for salvation. Long it seemed that his ambitions were beyond all hope, for no sign of the legendary source of immortality was found. Then, his aged body weakening from the onset of gradual illness, he received intelligence of a fiendishly defended site, hidden at the edge of the farthest continent of the most distant planet their boreholes could reach. It matched the myths in every particular; there could be no doubt this was the place.

His forces could not breach the site's perimeter. The emperor cared not, for the location was now revealed and his children would find a way in.

He summoned the princes and ordered them to bring him the Waters at the End of the Worlds, that he might be young again and rule for all eternity. Now, he would transmute his decrepit flesh into a form flawless and unkillable. He would wage terrible war upon every star that shone in every firmament until he drowned all possible universes in an infinite sea of blood.

His nine children swore their devotion and set forth upon their quest.

Even the least of the emperor's offspring went, the stunted Vallexiad, the one who was no good at fighting. As far as his father, the Emperor of Night, was concerned, sending him to breach lethal defenses was an excellent means of getting rid of him.

⁂

"It's the rocks that are the problem," said the legion general. "Can't get past them. They block boreholes."

Behind Vallexiad, his own borehole fizzled shut, the dimensional wound collapsing now he'd finished with it. Creating these tunnels through space-time was a gift of Wormkind.

Around him, in all directions save one, lay a desolate expanse that stretched to sullen mountains of purple stone. The exception to this bleak vista was straight ahead—a ring of tall gray stones, resembling the megaliths of primitive cultures.

"I assume they surround the Waters," Vallexiad asked the general. He repositioned his large satchel, careful not to let it fall to the stony ground. Its contents would not respond well to such treatment.

"Of course," interrupted his eldest brother, Dravinian, heir to the imperial throne. "They must be the defenses we heard about."

The general agreed, while another of Vallexiad's older brothers slithered over and prodded at his shoulder pack with one of his four arms. "What's this you carry in place of your sword or spear? Is it your lunch? What did you bring? Boiled human, grilled heart of servant? No, don't tell me, it's a green salad."

Vallexiad's eight siblings sniggered. The general, at least, had the decency to remain silent. Not all the legionaries followed his example.

"Some of my inventions," mumbled Vallexiad, embarrassed.

"Oh, dark gods of the abyss save us," snarled the heir apparent. "You need to learn how to handle a weapon. Skulking around in your playroom is not fit behavior for a Wormkind."

"Laboratory, not playroom."

Dravinian hissed with displeasure. "We stab our enemies, we cut their heads off, we wreak bloody mayhem. We do not tinker with bits of metal and wire." In disgust, the prince spat a glob of phlegm at Vallexiad's narrow belly and undulated his way back to the general.

Vallexiad listened as the crown prince interrogated the general regarding the site's fortifications and why the assembled legions hadn't made more headway. It transpired a significant number of the tall rocks were, in fact, legionaries who had attempted to storm the glade that ensconced the Waters. "They're turned to stone," repeated the general, lifting his muscular trunk off the stony ground with two of his four powerful arms and shuddering.

"How does that happen?" asked Vallexiad's next oldest brother, Barradhian.

"You're fine so long as you keep moving forward," explained the general. "At least, that's what we reckon. But the stones throw curses at you. Insults and the like. As soon as you turn to respond, you become one of them."

Dravinian let out a snort. "Hardly a barrier at all. Simple willpower is all that's called for here. Leave it to us, general. We'll be through before you know it."

Vallexiad heard the general mutter something under his breath. It sounded like, "It's harder than you think."

Prince Rappelvium, renowned for his accuracy with a spear, lasted three meters into the serried ranks of gray stones. As soon as he heard the taunt, "Can't even throw with proper form," he whirled about screeching, "Who said that?"

Three meters in and they were down a prince. So much for being superior to the legionaries.

Vallexiad concentrated on pushing his body forward.

Barradhian complained, "Was that a legionnaire saying that? Is he trying to ensnare us out of spite?" He shouted at the stones. "I order you to cut that out! Turned into rock you might be, but you are still under my command!"

"Hasn't lost any weight, has he?" shot back the stone next to him.

Incensed, Barradhian twisted about, opening his mouth to berate the rectangular chunk of rock. He never got the chance, becoming another one of them.

"I don't think they're loyal to us anymore," commented Vallexiad.

Crown Prince Dravinian, said, "Quite clever, this curse. We lose many more and all the approaches will be blocked with huge pieces of stone. It's a self-forming barrier."

"You think you're smart," sneered another rock.

"Yes, I do," agreed Dravinian without stopping. "You'll need to do better than that."

Brother Urglan, who'd called attention to Vallexiad's heavy satchel, fell to a remark about his unstylish chest armor. That left six. Dravinian didn't give the appearance of being upset. Vallexiad wasn't distraught, either. He didn't like his brothers.

In quick-fire order, three more of his siblings fell:

"What have you been crawling through? From that smell, I'd say mammal feces."

"How dare you—!" One.

"The only reason the emperor hasn't ordered your execution yet is because he can't remember your name for the warrant."

"I'll have you know my father honored me with new estates just last week—!" Two.

"You're running out of princes to hide behind. Must be worrying for such a despicable coward."

"I hide behind no one!" Three.

Vallexiad didn't pause to count. Nonetheless, he reckoned that left him, the crown prince, and Celynwall (originally fifth in line, but now second).

The rocks insulted him, too. He didn't react. Vallexiad was used to abuse. His entire life had been preparation for this moment.

He kept going and didn't look back.

●

On the far side of the rocks stood a forest. This enclave stood in stark contrast to the outer desolation. It was an oasis, impossible on a world otherwise devoid of vegetation.

The trio of surviving princes slithered through the trees. Vallexiad appreciated the soft carpet of grasses and moss. The forest soon gave way to a clearing, and at the heart of the clearing lay a pool of dark water.

The Waters at the End of the Worlds.

They were guarded.

A man sat under a single broad tree at the edge of the pool. A human. The ancient enemy of Wormkind.

He was clad in shining silver armor, with what seemed to be a shallow bowl at his side. Vallexiad wasn't certain, but he thought the man was dozing in the shade of the tree.

The crown prince snarled. "We claim these spring waters in the name of our father, the Emperor of Night, slayer of a hundred thousand civilizations across parallel time. Surrender or die."

The human blinked and stood. "Wormkinder," he said, using the term for Wormkind children, in their own language. He knew of them.

Celynwall drew his battle axes with his upper arms. "Mind your tongue or I'll hack it off."

"Why? It will merely grow back. A pointless exercise, all things considered."

"You've drunk the water, then?" Vallexiad gazed into the impenetrable oval of liquid, seeing nothing except an endless nothingness that chilled him as thoroughly as the void between planetary systems.

"A very long time ago. I cannot be killed. And I cannot be ignored."

"Ignored?" Dravinian had his weapon drawn as well: a war sword hewn from meteoric ore.

"My solemn duty is to explain the Riddle of the Waters. You can try not to listen. I can't stop you tying me up, what with there being three of you, and you being so large. But it wouldn't do you any good. Death abides here as well as life. Assuming you survive long enough, you'll beg me to explain eventually. You might as well pay attention now."

To Vallexiad's surprise, his brothers lowered their weapons.

The human nodded. "Very sensible. Now, you might wonder why the Waters are so lightly defended. The location is hidden, yes. The cursing stones surround us, yes. Nevertheless, you three made it. Therefore, it is clearly possible for searchers with sufficient determination and self-control to reach this point. The creators of this spring wanted not to keep its blessings to themselves but rather to grant those boons only to those best suited to them."

"There's a test," guessed Vallexiad. "To determine our worthiness."

"Your intelligence," corrected the human. "The First Ones didn't want stupid people drinking the Waters and cluttering up the universe with their idiocy forevermore."

"What is this test?" growled the crown prince.

"The Waters are poison unless consumed the correct way. They must be drunk from a particular cup."

"Doesn't seem difficult," responded the eldest brother.

The human lifted the bowl. Vallexiad saw it was not a cup or bowl at all. It was a sieve.

"Let me see if I understand." He straightened his satchel, masking the discomfort its weight caused. "We must consume the Waters using a vessel that cannot, by its very nature, hold liquid."

• •

"Lies! Deceit!" shouted Celynwall. He slithered to the edge of the pool. "Poison, indeed! I'm drinking straight from the source. I am Wormkind, your rules do not apply to me."

The pool bubbled for some minutes after Celynwall's body dissolved into nothingness.

The guardian shrugged. "As I said, it is death to drink the Waters from anything except this cup."

Dravinian shook his head. "My brother was right, this is trickery. A cup of holes is no cup at all. Use a cup I must, but not the one you offer." He cast about for a few moments, before finding a broad leaf on a nearby plant in the glade. He tore the leaf free. "I shall make my own drinking vessel. That shows intelligence."

With that, he dipped the frond into the Waters and lifted up a few droplets of moisture. Vallexiad watched as his eldest brother drank.

Death possessed a voracious appetite that day; the crown prince's body disintegrated in moments.

"That was not the solution," said the guardian.

Vallexiad considered leaving. As the new heir the empire would be his in due course. No, power wasn't enough—he wanted immortality.

The puzzle had a solution. One the guardian had found. The prince undulated around the pool and picked up the sieve. "This is a fine cup."

"Oh?" scoffed the guardian. "How will you drink from it?"

"With your help."

"I offer you no help."

Vallexiad was incapable of human expression. So, the guardian had no warning when the prince drew the experimental weapon from his shoulder pack.

"That looks like a giant crossbow," said the human. "Capable of firing multiple projectiles."

"I call it a boltlauncher," replied Vallexiad, and he shot the human six times.

・●・

"This cannot kill me," said the guardian, by way of a reminder. The bolts were long and thick. They'd struck the guardian in his arms, legs, and torso, impaling him firmly to the tree that had afforded him shade earlier.

"I do not seek your death."

"Then what is it you seek of me?"

"Your blood."

Vallexiad took the broad leaf his brother had used and filled its concave shape with the lifeblood dripping from the guardian's wounds. Next, he mixed the blood with dirt from beside the pool to form a glob of thick mud. Then, he took the mud and coated the base of the sieve with it. The Wormkinder picked more leaves and pressed them into the glue-like mixture, forming a water-resistant layer inside the sieve.

He filled the bowl with ease from the pool and flexed his snake-like torso into an upright posture, holding the cup aloft. The sieve did not leak.

The guardian frowned. "Does your father know how cunning you are?"

"No," replied the prince. "That will change." He drank the bowl's full measure. Warmth spread throughout his body, presaging his apotheosis.

Vallexiad let the sieve fall into the long grass. He didn't need it anymore.

●

The human grunted, failing to unpin himself from the tree trunk. "You've solved the riddle. Now, you can sprinkle some of that on your dead or transformed kin. A drop of the waters for each will restore them to normal life."

"I'm sure it would," agreed Vallexiad. "I have no intention of doing so."

The guardian blinked. "Only one other, save me, has found this glade and drunk the waters. He came long ago. He also made mud to seal up the sieve. I am relieved to say he used spit. His immortality achieved, he carried water in the bowl and sprinkled it upon the cursing rocks, restoring his predecessors to their natural forms. In that way, he was able to leave without walking through their deadly ranks. The Waters moved thereafter, to this new world, as they do whenever they are discovered, and my vigil recommenced. Since then, the ranks of cursing rocks have grown anew. I ask you then, if you do not intend to un-transform the rocks, how do you plan to leave? Immortal you may be, but you can still be transfigured."

Vallexiad rummaged in his pack and took out the other fruits of his scientific labors. "I call them 'grenades.'" He explained their purpose.

The guardian's eyes widened. "You could have used them to clear a safe path on the way in."

"True," replied Vallexiad, "but then more of my brothers would have made it this far."

• • •

Vallexiad slid from borehole to borehole, closing on the imperial palace. He imagined the pool had already relocated, transported through eldritch means to some new spot on a world unknown to Wormkind.

The emperor was waiting. His expression revealed he hadn't expected Vallexiad to be the one to return.

The Emperor of Night didn't mince words. "Have you brought me the Waters from the End of the Worlds?"

"Not exactly. I took them for myself."

Revenge was the emperor's credo. Still, Vallexiad wasn't afraid. His father couldn't kill him, so what retribution could he extract when all was said and done? Vallexiad needed only wait.

The cauldron of burning tar poured on his head caught Vallexiad unprepared. The pain was so intense and the tar so sticky he found he could not move. He'd trapped the guardian in the glade; his father had trapped him.

"Interesting. The damage heals. Still too weak to do much of anything, though, eh?" observed his father. The ancient warlord stared into his son's eyes. "You will give me what I want, one way or another."

•••

The next few rotations of the Wormworld about its black star brought Vallexiad no joy. The emperor directed his healers to drain blood from his only living son, in hopes of discovering and replicating the cause of his newfound immortality. Eternal life was not so easily analyzed. In due course, his healers announced failure.

In a rage, the emperor ordered Vallexiad's head cut off. No one protested—severing heads was a Wormkind tradition.

The Wormkinder lived on, though. In his undying state, Vallexiad was untroubled by anything so trivial as decapitation. Noticing that both parts of his son's body still endured, an idea came to the emperor.

He called for his healers again, those he hadn't had executed for incompetence, and bid them transplant his own head upon his son's body. His body was failing organ by organ, but here was an immortal frame with no owner. Why, the situation was perfect.

For Wormkind, the grafting of body parts was not the daunting challenge it was for other species. Vallexiad's severed head was positioned on a shelf with a good view; he saw the surgery, he witnessed the emperor's victory: The Emperor of Night possessed the unkillable form he'd always wanted—and wasted no time in commencing his war.

As for Vallexiad, his head was abandoned in a lightless dungeon.

• • •

In the absolute darkness of the tiny cell, Vallexiad had no way of telling how much time passed.

He was content to wait, and to plan.

His father, the great emperor, was a wily sort, but not blessed with tremendous intelligence.

His new body was immortal, undying, that was beyond question. Not the head, though. He could wage war all he liked, but the emperor couldn't avoid the reality that his brain was getting older. Sooner or later, it would succumb to disease or infirmity. Then, the empire would, quite literally, be without a head of state.

Fortunately, the emperor had one surviving heir, and an unkillable head could be reattached to an unkillable body. Such surgery was, after all, no great challenge for Wormkind.

Days turned to months and then, as Vallexiad had always known it would, the door to the cell opened.

"Bring me the master craftsmen," said the new Emperor of Night. "I have weapons of my own invention for them to produce in quantity. Unlike my father, I wage war with my mind. Ages stretch before me and I would fill them with fire."

Mike Morgan was born in London, but not in any of the interesting parts. He moved to Japan at the age of 30 and lived there for many years. Nowadays, he's based in Iowa, and enjoys family life with his wife and two young children. If you like his writing, be sure to follow him on Twitter where he goes by @CultTVMike or check out his website, PerpetualStateofMildPanic.wordpress.com.

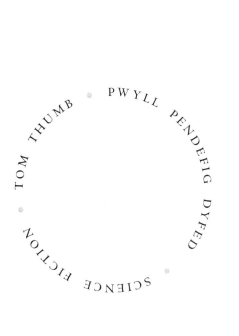

LITTLE TOM'S REALITY

REBECCA E. TREASURE

The wind had been blowing as long as Tom could remember. Sometimes, it made him cry. The endless howling outside the plastic dome he shared with his mom and dad peeled away at his insides.

Sometimes, it was like the soft blue blanket he tucked under his chin at night—always there, a comfort.

Today, it made him mad.

Tom looked up from the touchdesk to where his mom stood in the kitchen section of the round living area. "I just want to see outside. Just for a little bit."

He'd seen pictures, of course, and videos, and even walked through the VR landscape of the planet they called home.

But it wasn't the same.

His mother sighed, her hands clamping to her narrow waist like crocodile jaws. "How many times, Tom? It's too dangerous."

"I'll come right back in."

"We don't have a suit for someone as little as you. You can go outside when you're older. Finish your math." Shadow swallowed her face as she turned away.

Tom knew the truth. They'd never let him go outside.

He'd lived inside the four round windowless rooms of the house all his life. He knew he lived on Mars, he knew they were colonists from the planet Earth. He knew a lot of things from the videos and books, but he wanted to see Mars. He wanted to see other people.

Some days he thought only Mom and Dad and Little Tom were real in the whole universe.

Tom bent back to the math program on his touchdesk, tapping the sloth that moved along a branch to the number he needed. *Twelve plus seventeen is...* tap-tap-tap-tap-tap-tap. The sloth inched along to the sounds of his mother using air-jets to wash dishes and the screeching of the wind.

Mom put the last dish in the sterilizer and turned back to Tom, her face in the happy expression he preferred. "How about you set aside your math and spend some time in the VR?" Her bright voice made the anger grow in Tom's chest.

"I don't want to."

"Why not, honey? How about the rainforest today? You could look for a real sloth."

"It's *not* real. I want to see something *real*."

Her eyes flashed. "Tom, that's enough. We are very lucky to be the first colonists here, but there are costs."

"I don't care! I want to go outside!" Tom winced at the sound of stomps from behind him.

"How many times have I told you not to yell at your mother?" A fist seized him by the back of his shirt.

Dad dragged him out of the chair and let him go. Tom fell with a thump onto the grey carpet. His butt hurt, his ribs stung where the chair had scraped them.

Dad leaned down and yelled. "You show respect, damnit!"

"Yes, Dad." Tom looked down. He knew from long experience that meeting Dad's eyes only made the towering giant angrier.

If Tom kept his gaze on the floor, curled up small, sometimes Dad would stop. Sometimes Mom would say something.

"It's okay, dear." Mom didn't move forward. She held still when Dad got mad, too. "Tom just feels a little cooped up today."

"Too damn bad," Dad snarled. "It's dangerous."

"He knows." Her voice was chirpy, shrieking like the ravens in the VR Evergreen Forest. "He's only eight, after all."

Dad turned and stomped away.

Mom flashed back into her own anger. "Go to your room."

"Yes, Mom."

Laying on his bed, Tom screamed like the wind. They wouldn't bother him now.

'Feelings are real, Tom, let them out,' his Mom always said. What she meant was, keep them to yourself. They'd barely be able to hear him over the wind anyway.

He imagined his body turning inside out, following his voice into the air and then from the air filters into the world beyond.

His throat raw from the release, Tom curled up into a ball and slept.

He dreamed he wore a suit made just for him. He walked out of the airlock, as brave as a hyena charging into a crocodile-infested river. The danger didn't slow his steps, and he stood outside in the red wind. The horizon smeared in and out of sight through gaps in the flickering dust. Then, just like he promised, he turned around and went back inside.

I just wanted to see.

Tom opened his eyes. It was dark. Mom had pulled his blanket over him. Tom kicked it off and stood.

I just want to see.

He tiptoed to the bedroom door, his blanket trailing from a fist, and pulled it open. It hissed, and he waited. Sometimes

Mom stayed up late playing VR. Nothing. He crept across the living area to the airlock door.

His parents' suits hung on a rack, their helmets on shelves. Tom chewed his lip, his stomach hurting. If Dad caught him, Tom would be black and blue for a month. But maybe, just maybe, he could get outside and back in without them noticing.

That's all he wanted. He just wanted to look, see proof that the world he saw in VR was real. That would be enough.

Dad's suit would never fit. The giant dwarfed Little Tom. Tom slid his bare feet into Mom's boots, pulling the suit up around him. It sagged like elephant skin, so he stuffed his blanket around the gaping waist. He still struggled to get the zipper up to his chin because it kept catching where the suit bulged out. Tom reached for the helmet.

He dropped it. It thunked on the carpet and rolled away.

His breath caught, stopped at the top of his chest by the sudden slamming of his heart. His parents' door didn't open.

Tom scooped up the helmet. Rushing now, he pulled it over his head. He'd seen Mom latch it on a thousand times, and after two tries the suit sealed with a hiss. Air pumped along the back of his neck, and he shivered.

The suit smelled like Mom—soap and soil from the plants she studied. The wind faded away. Near silence filled Tom's brain. Tears filled his eyes. The quiet didn't feel real.

He turned to face the airlock door. The one door in the house he'd never been through. Tom almost fell when he took a step forward, the loose material around his legs catching and slowing him, but he managed. The airlock door swung open, just as it had a hundred times for Mom and Dad. Once he was through, once the airlock was cycling, they couldn't stop him.

Almost there.

Tom shuffled into the airlock, closed the door behind him, and slapped his floppy glove into the cycle button. The suit tried to inflate around him, but he didn't take up enough space, and it felt like a snake sliding over his skin as the material stretched.

Finally, the opposite door opened.

Eager, Tom slid his feet forward, keeping each leg straight to avoid the material tripping him.

That's weird.

The light coming from the end of the airlock was the same white-yellow as the lights inside his house. There wasn't any redness, no dust or wind.

Instead, as he reached the edge of the airlock, an open space met his eyes. White paths wound between lilac bushes and maple trees in dark brown soil. The sky above was made of glass. Beyond the glass, blackness pricked by white spots.

Tom stared up at the night sky, his eyebrows drawn and his lips threatening to pull into a frown.

This isn't Mars. It's just more inside.

Confused, Tom stumbled forward. The circular space was ringed by a dozen other airlocks, just like the one leading to his home. He didn't understand. Mom and Dad had warned him again and again about the dangers of the Martian surface on the other side of that airlock. Maybe they'd meant another airlock?

But no, if that was true, why couldn't he come into this beautiful space? It looked like a VR city park. There were benches, even, and a field of grass. Sure, the field wasn't any bigger than Tom's living area, but it was new and different. Why hadn't his parents let him see all this?

A girl with brown-bronze skin dropped out of one of the trees. She wore grey shorts and a grey t-shirt with "Meridiani Colony" printed on them, just like Tom was wearing under his

Mom's suit. The girl didn't have a helmet on, her curly hair mountainous and bouncy.

When she saw him, her head cocked and she skipped over. She was taller than Tom. Her mouth moved, and Tom stared at her. His arms tightened against his sides, the bulge of his blanket like a hug.

He reached up and, fumbling with the gloves, took off the helmet. The wind filled his ears again, but at a distance.

"What did you say?"

She poked at his suit. "Why are you wearing that?" She looked at him and her eyebrows drew together. "Who are you? I've never seen you before." The unfamiliar voice jangled in his ears.

"I'm Tom... Tom Pryderi."

"The Pryderis don't have any kids." She pursed her lips. "Where'd you come from?"

Tom didn't understand. His parents did have a kid. "I'm me. I've always been here."

She shook her head, curls flopping in front of her eyes. "Nuh-uh. There are only thirteen kids in Meridiani. You think I'd miss one?"

Thirteen kids? "How come..." Tom trailed off. He'd been about to ask her how come she didn't have a helmet on but that was stupid. He bit his lip and tried again. "How come I've never seen you before?"

She shrugged. "Don't you go to school?"

"My mom teaches me."

She shook her head again. Tom admired how the light glittered on her black hair. "All the kids learn from Mrs. Tinker."

"Tom, you get back here this instant!" The giant's voice filled the beautiful space, turning it to darkness and fear. Tom turned his head, his chest squeezing into his spine. The giant stormed toward him, unsuited.

The girl—Tom hadn't learned her name—gasped and took off running. Tom slammed the helmet on his head, hitched up the baggy pants with his fingers in loose gloves, and ran from his dad.

"Tom, come back!"

Tom ran. A bigger airlock caught his eye. Maybe that one led outside. He was in trouble now, but he wanted to see. He'd get beat for this, but he wanted to finish. If he could just see outside, this would all make sense.

The airlock door slid open, and Tom squeezed through the gap. He hammered at the eye-level cycle button and the door clicked shut. His breath tearing at his throat, Tom managed to get the helmet latched just as the airlock hissed.

Dad beat on the airlock window, his face red and raging. Tom moved away, down the long round hallway to the outer door.

This was what he'd expected to see. A wall of dust, glowing red in the light of the airlock. It consumed Tom as he ran to Mars, the howling louder than ever. The wind knocked him over, tossing him head over heels away from the airlock door.

Inside the flopping suit, Tom laughed.

Real. This is real.

He slammed into a boulder, maybe, or a building. It didn't matter—he couldn't see anything but a million specks of dust hammering into the faceplate of Mom's helmet. He couldn't fight the wind, couldn't even move his arms.

At least he'd done it. He'd gotten outside.

The dust buried him, swallowed him up. There in the belly of Mars, Tom examined his life. Outside the airlock of his house was a warm, welcoming place. A place with other kids, with trees and grass and a sky he could see. There was a school, a school that welcomed children. Why had his parents kept him inside? Why had they lied?

Tom had no answers. All he knew was that the Giant hurt him, Mom lied to him. That girl didn't know he'd existed.

The dust covered his faceplate now. Tom pulled his arms into the body of the suit and gripped his blanket.

I just wanted to see outside. I just wanted to see something real.

His parents wouldn't want him back. He knew the truth. And nobody else knew he was real. Maybe he'd just stay outside forever.

Eventually he slept.

Tom awoke surrounded by giants in suits. Narrow beams of white cut through the blowing dust, a spiderweb of light trapping him. Hands pulled him up out of the dust; a tall body scooped Tom up in strong arms.

Tom flailed—they'd take him back, he didn't want to go back.

Leave me alone! Let me be real!

The arms tightened and Tom let his body go limp. Sometimes that worked when Dad was angry. Dad would carry Tom back to his bed, leaving him alone.

Tom cried, the tears running down his neck to soak into his blanket. Mom and Dad were going to be so angry.

The person carried Tom back through the airlock and into the park space. Tom was gently set on his feet. The person knelt and reached out to unlock the helmet.

Trembling so hard he thought his teeth might crack, Tom tried to stop them.

Don't look, don't see me!

Someone else grabbed his arms, and the hands lifted Mom's helmet free of Tom's face.

"What the—"

Six adults in suits stared down at Tom. A woman with skin like the girl's, and a man whose black skin glistened with sweat like stars, a woman with hair the color of a VR wheat field, and the tall man who had carried Tom. Behind them stood Mom and Dad, their faces pale and their eyes wide.

They look as scared as me.

"Who are you?" The man who had carried Tom spoke in a quiet voice.

"I... I'm Tom. Tom Pryderi."

The four strangers turned to stare at Mom and Dad. Behind them, other people—families even, Tom saw more kids—had gathered. Their faces were stiff, stunned.

"What did you do, Tiernon?"

Dad shook his head, looking down.

Mom raised her chin. "It wasn't him. It was me. I forced him to keep the secret." Her voice wasn't bright, now. It was dark and full of tears.

The blonde woman spoke. "Who is he?" Her voice trembled and her hand reached out to Tom. "Is it Peter?"

Mom looked down, nodding. She began to cry.

Tom tried to get to his feet. "Mom, don't cry, I'm okay."

Mom sank to her knees. Dad's jaw ground back and forth. Tom looked away. He was in more trouble than he thought. What would these strange people do to him?

The blonde woman turned back, her eyes wide like she couldn't believe Tom existed.

Not real, not real.

"Tom... Tom, my name is Rhiannon. I'm..." She glanced back at Mom and Dad. "I was your mother. There was an accident, when you were a baby. The habitat lost pressure. We thought you'd been blown away, buried by the wind and the dust. We looked for you—" Her voice broke.

Tom looked between the woman and Mom. Mom sobbed. Disgust on the faces of the adults, rage on the tall man's face, the hope and sadness in the woman's... Tom didn't know what was real.

The other man spun. "You evil *bastards*. You kept this child hidden in your house for *eight years?*"

Mom spoke through her hands, which she'd pressed to her face. "Tiernon and I can't have children... the radiation storm... I found Peter after the decomp event. Rhiannon already thought he was lost. I... I brought him home." She pulled her hands away, staring at Tom. "We love you, Tom. Didn't we love you?"

Tom just stared at her. Nothing was real. Everything was as false as the VR rainforest.

The woman—Rhiannon—held out her hand to Tom. "Would you like to come home with me? It's... it's okay if you don't."

Tom cringed away from her. *Not real.*

He turned to the other people. "Was that your daughter earlier?"

The woman nodded, smiling, her eyes on Tom's. "She likes to climb the trees, but she's not supposed to. Frinda is always sneaking out at night."

"Can I come with you?" He didn't want to go back to his house, but he couldn't just go with a new Mom and Dad either.

Maybe someday, but tonight he wanted someplace safe. The girl had been nice. He wanted to talk to her. Maybe a kid would know what was real.

The woman glanced at Rhiannon, who nodded. "Sure, Pe... Tom. My name is Amidia. We'd be happy to have you."

Amidia lifted Tom free of the suit. When she set him down, he pulled his blanket up to his chin.

Rhiannon cried out. "It's his, it's Peter's blanket."

Tom wanted to tell her it wasn't Peter's, it was Little Tom's, but that wasn't real either. "It's just mine," he whispered.

The tall man turned back to Tom. His jaw was tight, his eyes sharp. Tom looked away from him. Then the man knelt. "Tom, I'm your father. I know you don't remember us, but we've missed you so much."

Tom looked up. The man's eyes were soft, sparkling with tears even. Tom sighed in relief—the anger wasn't for him. Tom nodded, unsure what else to do.

"When you're ready, we'll be here."

"I'll get him back to our house," Amidia said. "He must be exhausted."

Tom followed her, his blanket over his shoulder. Behind him, shouting started.

Tom focused on the wind. It was real. The wind had always been real.

Rebecca E. Treasure grew up reading science fiction in the foothills of the Rocky Mountains. She received a degree in history from the University of Arkansas and a Masters degree from the University of Denver. After graduate school, she began writing fiction. Rebecca has lived many places, including the Gulf Coast of Mississippi and Tokyo, Japan. Her short fiction appears in the anthology *A Dying Planet* from Flame Tree Publishing and will appear in the forthcoming *Hold Your Fire* anthology from WordFire Press. She was a recipient of the 2020 Superstars Writing Seminar scholarship. She currently resides in Texas Hill Country with her husband, where she juggles two children, a corgi, a violin studio, and writing. She only drops the children occasionally.

THE TWELVE MONTHS · DIAMONDS AND TOADS · HUMOR/FANTASY

DIAMONDS, TOADS, AND... PUMPKINS?

MELISSA MEAD

Marta slapped another layer of tape over her mouth. Outside the cottage, poor Bessie lowed to be milked. The poor thing had to be uncomfortable, but Marta didn't dare to venture outside untaped in her current state. She always sang while milking. If she forgot herself, Bessie's stall would be ankle deep in diamonds and rubies before the bucket was half full.

Bessie mooed again-and someone knocked on the door.

"Oh!" said Marta. The tape, with a garnet stuck to it, ripped loose.

"Ow!" Marta exclaimed. She flung the tape away and spat out a topaz. The knocking got louder. Marta shut her lips tight and ran to open the door.

Constable Peterson's son, Peter, stood on the front step, shifting from foot to foot.

"Um, 'morning, Miss. Is Widow Andersen in? Or Miss Fanny?"

Marta shook her head and tried to look calm, even though her heart started pounding at the mention of her stepmother and stepsister. If she hadn't been so terrified, she would have wanted to slap Peter for not recognizing her. Then again, Peter had never been bright. Good looking, and strong as an ox, but not much brighter than one, either.

"Well, Miss, it's just that, well, no one's seen them for days, and there's all these toads and snakes out here, which isn't right, what with the snow and all, and, well, after that incident with the rats and that piper fella last month, well, folks are talking witchcraft."

Marta shook her head again and tried to back away, but Peter had caught a glimpse of the glittering piles on the table behind her.

"Great Mother Goose!" he exclaimed, pushing past Marta to touch the emeralds, diamonds and sapphires on the table. "They're real. They're all real." He turned back to Marta with a stern look on his face (and a few jewels in his pockets. For evidence, he said.) "All right, Miss. Something funny's going on here. Tell me the whole story."

Resigned, Marta went to fetch a basin.

"What are you doing? Spit it out!"

"It" proved to be a flawless opal, soon joined by an amethyst, an aquamarine, and then a veritable flood of jewels, dropping from Marta's lips with every sentence she spoke.

"Shame on you, Peter Peterson! Don't you know your old friends? After all the times we played hide-and-seek in Farmer McDonald's pumpkin patch, how could you mistake me for my stepmother's housemaid? Especially since we haven't HAD a housemaid here, ever?"

"Marta?" he said, staring in disbelief at the gems pouring from his old playmate's mouth. "They said you went queer in the head after your parents died, and you'd been sent to Madame Primula's School for Damsels in Distress."

Marta choked, and almost swallowed a turquoise. "I've been distressed all right, ever since Father married that woman and brought her daughter here." Marta sighed and swirled the rainbow of gems in the basin. "Sit down and I'll tell you about it."

Peter sat. Marta offered him a bowl of stewed pumpkin. It was the only thing left in the larder, but Peter had always had an odd fondness for the stuff.

"Wash your hands first," said Marta, with a mischievous smile. "Remember where those rubies you were handling came from."

Peter looked nauseated, and scrubbed his hands raw before he dug into the bowl of pumpkin mush. Marta emptied the jewels into the washtub, sat, and settled the basin on her lap.

"I was so glad when Fanny and her mother moved in. I thought it would be nice to have a sister. Well, Fanny was the one who ended up thinking it was wonderful, because now she had someone to mend her clothes, do the sweeping, and generally lord it over."

"But your father…"

"Believed everything my stepmother said, even when she said that Widowmaker Valley sounded like the perfect spot for a picnic." Marta looked away from her questioner. Pearls spilled into the basin like milky tears. "She told him to go on ahead in the horse-cart, and that she'd walk behind, because she needed the exercise." Marta sniffled. "I think Father got more exercise than she did, at least until the Dragon of Widowmaker Valley caught up with him. And then my stepmother told me that hard work builds character. She obviously believed that Fanny had enough character already."

"Oh, she was a character all right!" said Peter, nodding vigorously. "After what she said to me…" Peter leaned close enough for Marta to feel his hot, squash-scented breath on her ear, lowered his voice half a decibel to what he no doubt thought was a conspiratorial whisper, and said "Can you believe that she told me that she didn't like stewed pumpkin?"

"Imagine that," said Marta, after a long pause. A bit of quartz pattered into the basin.

"So where have they both gone? And what's happened to you? You never used to spit sapphires, just pumpkin seeds. You've got a diamond chip stuck between your teeth, by the way."

"Thanks. Anyway, life went downhill from there. And before you start going on about 'wicked stepmothers,' and shaking your head…"

Peter stopped shaking his head.

"Fanny was the real brains behind it all. Not that Widow Andersen wasn't bad enough, but she was mostly just self-centered and cranky. You know: 'Put another log on the fire, girl. My feet are cold.' 'You call this porridge? I wouldn't feed this to a bear!' That kind of thing. But she didn't go out of her way to make me miserable, the way that Fanny did. Fanny was the one who put dried peas in my bed to prove that I was 'spoiled' when I couldn't sleep, and used my breakfast milk to wash her face in-as though anything could improve THAT complexion! That wasn't the worst of it, though. At least you can stew peas, and poor old Bessie always did give enough milk for two cows. But last month we heard about the January Ball at the squire's house. Fanny insisted that she was going, of course."

"The ball was yesterday," Peter pointed out. "And Fanny and her mother weren't there."

"Yes, I know," said Marta patiently. "I wasn't either, and I'm about to tell you why. Have some more pumpkin."

Peter dug into his second bowl of mush, and Marta emptied out the basin.

"Fanny spent the last of what was supposed to have been my dowry on a new dress for the ball. Purple velvet, of all things. She laced herself so tightly that her face almost matched the dress. She looked like an overripe plum, only with lace trim. Then she said that she had to have a corsage of fresh violets to go with it."

Peter blinked and looked out the window. "Kinda snowy for violets."

"That's what I told her," said Marta. She emptied the basin again and sat down. "You aren't going to believe this," she warned Peter. "I expect you'll have me taken to the asylum or something once I tell you, assuming you don't have me burnt for witchcraft." She gave Peter a questioning, hopeful look, but his eyes were fixed on the tourmaline and moonstone at the bottom of the basin. So much for any hope of him having a fit of chivalry and promising to defend her. Marta sighed and told her story, to the accompaniment of pattering gems:

●

"There aren't any violets this time of year, Fanny dear," said Marta in her gentlest, most conciliatory voice. "It's winter. And I'm just about to go fetch water from the well."

"I know it's winter, you stupid cow!" Fanny bellowed. "That's when you're SUPPOSED to have a New Year's ball."

"Oh, my head," Widow Andersen moaned.

"And I got my perfectly elegant violet dress just FOR this ball!"

"Oh, my poor head!" whimpered the widow.

"It's a violet dress, and it needs violets!" Fanny's howl shook the windows.

"Oh, my poor, aching head! Get those violets for my daughter this minute, girl!"

"But Stepmother, we're out of water, and I need to go to the well for more. So Fanny can wash up for the ball."

"What do you think milk is for? You heard her! Get me my violets!" Fanny was a big girl, and beneath her soft exterior lay the muscles of a blacksmith. And, Marta reflected as Fanny carried her bodily to the door and flung her into a snowdrift, a lump of cold iron where her heart should've been.

Marta didn't waste time pounding on the door and shouting to be let back in. She had about as much chance of that as her father had had against the dragon. At least dragonfire would have been warmer. The January wind blew straight through Marta's paper-thin dress. Not wanting to freeze solid just outside her own front door, she marched briskly toward the warm barn.

The wind increased tenfold, and snow blew around her until she couldn't see the house at her back or anything in front of her. She walked in the direction that she hoped was forward.

It wasn't.

Nor was it backward, because she didn't reach the house again. She walked until she couldn't feel her feet. If she could have, she would have realized that she was going uphill. Which was strange, considering that she lived in a town so flat that the streams needed a push to start flowing. But she was climbing all the same, up a wooded mountainside. The higher she climbed the more the snow thinned, until she found herself standing on the hilltop, staring at a blazing bonfire.

Once her face thawed out enough for her to blink, she noticed the men around the bonfire. Twelve of them: three in white robes, three in green, three in gold and three in brown. The oldest, a bearded man in white robes, turned to Marta.

"What do you wish, Daughter?" he asked.

Marta was pretty sure this imposing gentleman was no relative, but she managed to stammer out "M-my stepsister has sent me for violets, Sir. If I don't come back with them, she'll bench-press me."

The old man frowned, and said "Brother March, this is your department."

A young man in green stepped forth and touched the ground. The snow melted, and a cluster of fragrant violets sprang up. At Brother March's nod she picked them, bowed to her strange benefactors, and ran home.

⁕●⁕

"How about pumpkins? Could this March guy do pumpkins?" Peter interrupted.

Poor Bessie mooed urgently from the barn.

"March isn't pumpkin season," said Martha shortly. She glanced toward the barn, eyed the overflowing basin, and decided to give him the condensed version. Especially since the flood of jewels was starting to chip her dental enamel. She gave Peter another scoop of pumpkin and went on:

⁕●⁕

"So I gave Fanny the violets, but then she wanted strawberries, and back into the snowdrift I went. So I retraced my steps, or at least made my best guess. The gentlemen were still there, and Brother June stepped forward and grew the most amazing strawberries… and no, pumpkins aren't a summer thing either."

"So I gave Fanny the strawberries, but then she HAD to have apple pie, 'With GOOD apples, not those old wrinkly things in the cellar,'" so I headed out before she could toss me into the snowdrift again…"

⁕●⁕

"And a guy from Fall gave you apples and pumpkins!" said Peter triumphantly, holding up his empty bowl like a victor's chalice. Marta sighed and refilled it.

"Not exactly. Pumpkins are more of an October thing, really. And, well, Brother September was about to help, but then this old woman in a patchwork gown turned up, leaning on a stick with a wooden goose head on top." Marta realized that there was no simple explanation for this business, and resigned herself to telling the whole tale, warts, toads, and all:

• • •

"January, you old coot!" the old woman bellowed. "Have you and your brothers been stealing my protagonists again?"

Brothers February through December winced, and even January looked shaken, but he drew himself up and replied with dignity.

"By the Pen of Perrault and the Library of Lang I swear to you, Mother, that the girl came to us as foretold, and we have played our parts as written."

"Hmph." She turned her backs on them and shook a crabbed finger at Marta. "Why didn't you go to the well like you were supposed to? I've been sitting next to it for the last forty-eight hours! On a damp log. And then when you didn't show up I had to hike all the way up here- really, what kind of operation are we running? The lack of inter-story coordination is appalling."

The Months muttered variations of "Sorry, Mother," and "Beg pardon, Mrs. Goose, Ma'am," and shuffled their feet.

"Mrs. Goose? You're Great Mother Goose herself?" Marta sank into a curtsey. "I'm so sorry. I would've told Fanny to go get her own violets if I'd known you were expecting me to fetch water right then."

"Finally, something's going right!" The old woman smiled and patted Marta on the cheek. "Good girl. Polite and respectful, just like the story says." You shall be rewarded. There, that's one bit down." She took Marta's hand in a firm grip. "This is highly irregular, but I'm running late, so we'll have to settle for an abridged version." She glanced back at the cowering Months and said "And then we'll have a talk."

⁂

"You met Great Mother Goose herself?" Peter sat with a spoonful of pumpkin forgotten halfway to his mouth. "No way!"

Marta nodded and went on:

⁂

In a blink, Marta and Mother Goose were standing in front of Marta's cottage.

"What happened?" said Marta, and two bits of rose quartz fell from her mouth.

"Standard reward for virtue, my dear. Now, about this stepsister of yours..."

Mother Goose rapped on the door with her stick. Fanny opened it, took in her visitor's wrinkled face and patched dress, and said "Yeah? What do you want, old bat?"

"Concise. Saves me time. Just for that, I'll make sure none of them are venomous." She slapped Fanny's cheek and shouted "Be punished for your rudeness!"

"Hey!" Fanny shouted, and a corn snake slithered from her mouth. Fanny tried to scream and throw up at the same time. It sounded like somebody choking on a toad.

"What are you doing to my poor sweet baby?" Widow Andersen rushed up, batting feebly at Mother Goose.

"Ohh, that's not good," Peter mumbled through a mouthful of pumpkin.

"That's nothing compared to what Fanny did," Marta replied. "Hauled off and kicked her in the shin."

"That's REALLY not good."

"No kidding. Fanny was struggling and swearing. Horned toads were flying everywhere. Great Mother Goose grabbed her arm, and she cussed a boa constrictor. Then Widow Andersen grabbed her other arm, and they were hauling her back and forth, with Fanny spitting garter snakes the whole time. I shouted 'Don't hurt her!,' because, well, she's a sadist, but I didn't want to watch her get ripped in half. Did you know Widow Andersen's surprisingly wiry?"

Then Great Mother Goose said "Enough of this! I'm behind schedule." She looked me right in the eye and said "Because you spoke up on this ungrateful girl's behalf, know that I shall keep these two for a fortnight as my servants. Then they shall return."

"Nice of her to reassure you like that."

"Reassure? That was a warning! I've got two weeks to pack up and get out. Do you have any idea the temper Fanny'll be in once she's been made to do housework? But I can't leave poor old Bessie behind, unmilked. Not to mention Fanny'd probably make her into steak, just out of spite."

Peter bowed his head, staring mournfully into the empty pumpkin bowl. "This is awful."

"Well, it's not so bad now that you're here. If you'd be willing…"

"Say no more." Peter stood up, his face grim with determination. Marta wondered if she'd misjudged him. He marched out the door, toward the barn… and kept going.

"What about Bessie?" Marta shouted. "Where are you going?"

"To find that Brother October guy!" Don't worry; Marta; I'll make sure you have plenty of pumpkin for your journey!" He took a step uphill, even though the ground was as flat as, well, a mashed pumpkin, and vanished.

Marta stood staring after him. She cursed a small onyx, and headed back toward the house.

It wasn't so bad, she mused silently. She was pretty sure the Brother Months wouldn't let an innocent like Peter come to harm. The Constable was bound to come looking for his son when Peter didn't come home for dinner. By that point, Peter would be back, sitting at her kitchen table with a load of pumpkins.

She left a note on the table for the Constable. He'd take good care of Bessie. He had more sense than his son.

Who was…kind of sweet, in his addle-pated way. Marta left her grandmother's pumpkin mush recipe next to the note for Peter Senior.

Then she taped her mouth shut and, careful not to step on the frozen toads, went out to milk the cow.

Melissa Mead lives in Upstate NY. She's the author of the *Twisted Fairytale* Flash series at Daily Science Fiction and several fairy tale retellings in the *Sword and Sorceress* anthologies, among other things. Her Web page is carpelibris.wordpress.com.

BEAUTY AND THE BEAST · THE GOLEM OF PRAGUE · FANTASY

THE RABBI'S DAUGHTER AND THE GOLEM

ALEX LANGER

The long walkway loomed in front of Rokhl, crisscrossed by the shadows of waving willow trees. She hugged herself tight to hold her shaking body together.

Feet, please, another step. Heart, maybe try to beat less loudly.

She dragged herself up towards the tall black doors one trembling step at a time, spring frost under her feet.

No one had entered the synagogue's grounds for three years. Not since her father, Rabbi Loew, had vanished like a morning fog after months of candle-lit nights in its attic. She missed him terribly, an empty space in her heart that gathered cobwebs. Cryptic notes scribbled on parchment in his dust-filled study — *I have become an instrument of Creation, of deathless life*, one read — mocked her.

Yet at her mother's prohibition, she had never gone searching for him. But now, with the woman bedridden and wilting, Rokhl had kissed her and slipped away. She could not live without either of them, and her mother and father deserved a chance to say goodbye.

The doors swung open into near-darkness, afternoon sunlight dripping through grime-covered windows.

"*Tate*? Papa?" she called out, her voice echoing against the empty stone walls. There was nothing in the sanctuary but the smell of decay and the skitter of rats. The dilapidation wrenched at her heart. She had spent so many days of prayer and community and laughter here, and now it was a desolate ruin. The Emperor had ordered it closed, and the Jews of Prague obeyed. It was haunted by evil spirits, some whispered, or cursed by Lilith herself. She feared what she would find, and even more what she might not.

Rokhl felt her way towards the stairs. Her stomach clenched from fear as she climbed. Wrapping her hand tightly around her good-luck amulet, she tip-toed down the musty hall to the final stairway, leading to the geniza. She climbed the darkened stair, and opened the door.

As her eyes adjusted, she could see papers scattered over the floor, reams of refuse inscribed with the name of HaShem.

"*Tate*? Are you there?"

"Rokhl?" she heard a familiar voice croak in disbelief. Her heart surged. She had hoped against hope that she might hear that voice again. "*Tate!*" she shouted joyously, then felt an iron grip over her mouth.

"You don't belong here," a voice said in her ear, raspy and brittle. Its bearer spun her around and shoved her hard, and she crashed against the wall.

"Who are you?" Rokhl cried.

The shadowy figure did not reply. He was tall and hulking, and very still. He turned and left, slamming the door and leaving them in pitch-darkness.

Rokhl crawled in the direction of her father's voice. "*Tate*, are you hurt?" she said.

"No, my love," he replied shakily.

She felt towards him and touched his wrist. It felt bony and frail. Three years of captivity, she thought. Then, the fear began to creep in past the joy and righteous anger. "What was that *thing?*" she asked.

Her father didn't answer. "Rokhl," he started, "you shouldn't have come."

Rokhl opened her mouth to respond when the door swung open, bringing with it a burning lamp. The room was lit with a dim glow, and Rokhl could finally see her father's captor.

She screamed.

The broad figure was the shape of a man, roughly. Its face was greyish clay, with a misshapen, bulbous nose, a thin-lipped slash for a mouth, and smooth stones for eyes. Hebrew letters were inscribed on its forehead: *alef-mem-taf*, spelling *emet*, truth. "Whoever you are, let my father go!" she cried, shrinking away in terror.

The golem growled. "My creator is here to stay, until he fulfils his promise," it said.

Rokhl turned to her hollow-cheeked father, whose beard had grown tangled and white. "*Tate?*" she whimpered.

"It's true," her father said forlornly, then grew angry. "But I will not!"

Rokhl's heart shuddered with panic and love. Before she could consider it, her mouth opened and she shouted. "Let me take his place!"

"You are brave," the golem said. "Rav, do you accept?"

Rokhl's father shook his head madly. "Of course not!"

The golem made a grotesque mockery of a smile. "Well, I do," it said. "Maybe now you will do justice."

The moving statue hauled Rabbi Loew over its shoulder. As her father went limp, Rokhl struggled to pull him down, but the beast shrugged her off, carried him out of the geniza, and slammed the door.

Rokhl didn't cry for help. She knew in her bones that it would do no good. Nor did she sleep, terror and success at freeing her father and uncertainty making her heart race in the darkness. But, as morning came, for the first time since her arrival, Rokhl began to weep.

• • •

That afternoon, the golem allowed her to leave the geniza.

When she shrank away from the open door, it stood still. The golem did not seem to want to harm her. "You said you would take your father's place. Please don't break your promise to me," it quaked. She was afraid, but its manner seemed…innocent, almost child-like. Seizing the opportunity, she scampered down the stairs.

Rokhl found shelter in the synagogue's library. It was cramped and overflowing with books and chaotic piles of her father's notes, but the smell of paper and leather felt safe in a frightening, alien world. And unlike at home, when there was always a crisis to address or someone to care for, she had time to read. Her father insisted that his daughter be educated, to hold court for her future husband, a great rabbi, he would say proudly. Rokhl looked at the floor when he said that: she loved study for its own sake, unwinding the knotted mysteries of the Sages to learn how to live a virtuous life.

The golem, meanwhile, left her alone. Most of the time, she would not have known it haunted the synagogue, other than the jugs of water and loaves of bread it left outside the library a few times a day. One morning, after falling asleep on the hard floor, she found a straw mattress lying against the wall.

Two weeks after coming to find her father, she looked up to find the golem watching her from the threshold. Despite its size, it was stealthy, its footsteps nearly silent. Its blank features suggested sadness, although she did not know if the golem truly felt.

"May I enter?" the golem asked formally. Rokhl nodded, and her curiosity prompted a question.

"What should I call you?" Rokhl asked.

"I have no name," it said, after a long pause.

"No name?" Rokhl echoed, surprised.

"Your father did not give me one," it said bitterly. "Nor can I read and write to choose one of my own."

How could it not have a name? It might not be a man, but it spoke and moved. Even pets had names. And if it thought, could it not study Torah? How else would it know to follow the path of righteousness? Of course it had locked up her father: it didn't know better.

Rokhl pondered. "How about Adam? He too was sculpted from clay."

The golem looked at her. Its round stone eyes seemed to widen. "Yes, I would like that," it said quietly.

Rokhl returned to reading, but knowing the golem's eyes were on her, she couldn't concentrate. "Do you want something, Adam?" she asked.

The golem's mouth shivered as it paused. "To read and write. Would you teach me?" it finally said.

Rokhl's heart quivered. Her captor still terrified her, but there was something pleading and pure in its voice. And how could she say no? The golem had not been taught right from wrong. Perhaps, she thought, it would let her go if she did.

"Come sit," she said, patting a space on the floor. The golem obeyed, gently moving volumes of Talmud aside. Where to begin, Rokhl thought, and then it struck her. Its name.

"Adam," she said, "is spelled like this," drawing the letters in the collected dust of the floor. *Aleph-dalet-mem sofit*. The golem watched, rapt.

Their first lesson lasted until their candles burned down to stubs.

• • •

The golem brought her an inkwell and paper to write. She wasn't sure where the golem got them from. The golem told her it stole them in the night, like the food she lived on. Rokhl found a half-full coin-purse and pressed it to Adam's hands. Leave one of these when you take things, otherwise you are breaking a promise, she told the golem.

As the days grew longer, Rokhl found her fear fading, replaced with a surprising contentment. There was a purity and simplicity to life here, even as she missed her family and friends terribly.

They sat, studying in the evening's dying light. The golem had improved rapidly. When it learned something new, it would make a noise like cracking pottery, which Rokhl soon realized was laughter. She started to love that sound.

They paused for Rokhl to stretch. When she sat back down, the golem shifted uncomfortably, and asked, "Rokhl, what is Shabbos?"

Rokhl pondered. How to explain Shabbos? It was like breathing, so integral that it was hard to describe. She cleared her throat.

"When HaShem created the heavens and the earth, he saw that it was good, and rested. We sanctify that day by separating it from the week. In resting, we are that much closer to HaShem," she said, hoping she had been clear.

The golem peered at the floor. "I worked every day for your father. I would do things for him when he couldn't because it was Shabbos," it said.

Rokhl's heart fluttered. Make Adam work on Shabbos? Without a servant's due payment? She did not want to believe her father would mistreat his creation such, but something told her that it was telling the truth. Adam was gentle, simple. It wouldn't lie. After all, how would he—it—know how?

"I'm sorry, Adam. He shouldn't have done that," Rokhl said.

The golem looked at Rokhl with its pebble eyes and asked, "Could you...make Shabbos?"

Rokhl smiled, and agreed.

That Friday evening, Rokhl washed her face and changed into a clean dress that the golem had brought her: it fit surprisingly well. She untangled and braided her hair as best she could. Per her instruction, the golem had brought challah and wine.

As Rokhl lit and blessed the candles, the golem stood in the corner, bathed in sunlight. It was not a handsome sculpture, but there was an elegance to its form. She waved her hands over the flames and covered her eyes, saying the blessing. She could feel the golem watching her with wonder.

Next, she poured a cup of wine. "Adam, repeat after me. *Baruch atah HaShem.*"

"*Baruch atah HaShem,*" the golem said, stumbling over the words.

"*Eloheinu Melech haolam,*" she said.

"*Eloheinu Melech haolam,*" it said.

"*Borei p'ri hagafen,*" she said.

"*Borei p'ri hagafen,*" he said. Blessed are You, HaShem our God, Sovereign of the World, Creator of the fruit of the vine.

The golem did not eat or drink, so after saying the rest of the prayer, Rokhl took a long draught of the wine. After eating little but bread and fruit, it overwhelmed her senses, leaving her head adaze. She moved onto the challah, sprinkling it with salt.

She reached her hand out to touch the braided loaf, and the golem did the same. Their fingers brushed against each other for a moment, and Rokhl shivered, and pulled away.

Baruch atah HaShem, Eloheinu Melech haolam, haMotzi lechem min haaretz. Blessed are You, HaShem our God, Sovereign of the World, who brings forth bread from the earth.

Rokhl ate, and drank. She sat near the window, head buzzing pleasantly, as the sun descended and the stars rose. As she did, Adam sat next to her. He reached out, and their fingers intertwined. This time, Rokhl did not let go.

• • •

Shabbos became their weekly tradition. Between teaching and rest, Rokhl dove into her father's notes, and organized them as best she could. They were scrawled drawings and numerological formulas in Hebrew and Aramaic, fragments of spells and stray thoughts about the nature of the divine. A few times, Rokhl slipped out of the synagogue at night to walk the grounds. But something held her here. She no longer wanted to leave. Here, she was far away from the warm, suffocating embrace of her father and his genius, away from the interruptions or obligations of family life.

And even as her heart sometimes twinged with homesickness, doubt clouded her mind. Why had her father created Adam? He was not HaShem. What had given him the hubris to behave like he was?

Her dreams became vivid, twisted landscapes, valleys of awoken bones and heat from the furnaces of Gehenna. She saw her father, screaming in agony as flames licked his body. As she came closer, his face twisted and bent, his mouth becoming a slash, his flesh baking and cracking, his eyes melting into smooth, round stones.

Rokhl sputtered awake. She could feel her cheek stained with ink from the parchment in front of her. The golem stood in the doorway of the library, watching her silently. Candle-light flickered against its statue-like face. A question burned against her tongue.

"What did my father promise you?" she asked.

The golem sat. "He made me a servant, and promised that he would make me into a real man one day," the golem said quietly. "But after countless nights locked away in that attic, when I demanded that he honor that promise, he refused. He said it would be an abomination. So I kept him here until he would."

Rokhl's chest tightened at the betrayal her father had wrought. She did not recognize the man the golem described, but she knew it told the truth.

"You are not your father. You have been so kind to me," the golem said. "You may leave, if you so choose. Or perhaps he will return for you."

Rokhl's heart broke for the golem. What had he—it—done to deserve this? "Can I fulfill my father's promise?" she asked, plaintively.

The golem shrugged. "I don't know. Even if I did, I would not know how. But Rokhl, I am caged by this building even more than you. If I cannot ever taste the world as it is meant to be, if you cannot find a way to free me, I would rather be destroyed than go on like this."

Rokhl felt her tears gather. "All you need to do to destroy me is wipe away this *aleph*," the golem said, gesturing at its forehead. "Your father told me that much, whenever I did not perform to his expectations. Turn *emet*, truth, to *met*, death, and I will crumble as surely as paper burns in a fire."

Rokhl began to sob at the injustice her father had wrought, and the sweet being he had made into a monster. As she did, the golem held her. Its arms encircled her gently. "I will find a way," she whispered. "Give me a week, I will find a way."

• • •

The next Shabbos, she lit the candles and sipped the wine. Adam said the blessings with confidence, and took her hand over the bread. While other weeks, she had dabbed wine on the golem's lips as a joke, to tinkling laughter, this week was solemn. As the sun fell behind the horizon, she turned to her erstwhile captor.

"Are you ready?" she asked.

The golem nodded. "I am," Adam said, and stepped towards her. It kneeled in front of her, and closed its eyes. Even kneeling, the golem came up to the top of Rokhl's chest.

Rokhl stepped closer. She had worked tirelessly through her father's notes, burning through their candles as she stayed awake into the night. She was no great scholar, but determination made up for a lack of genius, she hoped.

Rokhl took a deep breath, and prayed. What she planned may be an abomination, she thought, but only this would repair the greater crime her father had committed. It was one thing to make a man with magic. It was another to deny such a man his personhood, to make a slave and justify it as holy. That was the true perversion of Creation.

Was it right? The Law might say otherwise.

She looked at Adam, and thought, *damn the Law*.

Rokhl dipped her finger in the melting wax of the Shabbos candle, wincing at the pain. She bent down, and brushed her hand against the golem's forehead, then brought it down to its chest. Over its heart, she drew two letters: *chet* and *yud*. It spelled *chai*, life. Then, she lifted the golem's face, and kissed its lips. She tasted the clay, bitter and cool, then pulled away.

Nothing happened at first, and Rokhl's heart thudded with despair. Then, the golem began to twitch. It fell backwards onto the floor, shivering. Rokhl watched in amazement as the spell worked. The golem's rough-hewn feet cracked and shattered and emerged as golden-brown skin with delicate black hair. The transformation worked its way up its legs and arms, then torso. Its face broke apart, thin lips remaining, with a rounded curve of a nose. Its eyes were the last to change, emerging as warm, dark-brown spheres.

The golem lay gasping for air. It—he—continued to shake. Rokhl knelt next to him, with a cup of water. He drank greedily after a moment, and then coughed and sputtered and sat up. He looked at her, then himself.

"Rokhl?" he said, overwhelming excitement and fear dueling in his voice.

Rokhl kissed him again. This time, he tasted sweet, like a person should. When she finally pulled away, she smiled.

"Adam," she said. "There is so much for you to see."

Alex Langer is a Canadian Jewish writer and law student. He grew up in Toronto, and now lives in Brooklyn, NY with his fiancée and cat. His short fiction has appeared in *Dream of Shadows,* and is upcoming in the *AURELIA LEO Originals Anthology* Volume I. You can find his takes at @AlexLanger1993 on Twitter.

THE NIGHTINGALE • IRON JOHN • STEAMPUNK

ABIGAIL WASHINGTON AND THE ANGELIC ORGAN OF FAR KHITAN

JOSHUA GAGE

The town of New Bethany wasn't so much a town, as a street between two hills. The main feature was Reverend Solomon Hazard's Cross of Redemption Temple, a white church on top of the hill on the north side of town that towered over the citizens of New Bethany and drew them to worship on the Sabbath. And while Reverend Hazard's sermons were potent and fiery, everyone knew that what drew the congregation and held them rapt in their seats was the voice of Abigail Washington.

Nobody knew where Abigail Washington had come from, or even how she managed to get into town without a steam carriage bringing her, but one day, there she was, a small child with matted hair and layers of dirt covering her dark skin, rags barely clinging to her body, hand out for any coin or scrap of food that the few people wandering through town would offer her. While New Bethany was no stranger to beggars or vagrants, this was a child, and the people who frequented New Bethany would complain loudly to each other that someone should do something. Eventually, Reverend Hazard agreed that he would take on this charge, and so he did. He raised Abigail in the church, and taught her to read and write from scripture, and taught her how to sing from the hymnal. The church ladies' auxiliary would bring her clothes, and taught her rudimentary cooking and cleaning skills, so that by the time Abigail was a young woman of fourteen, she was able to tend to herself. Reverend Hazard had set her up in a small one room shack behind the church, and donations to the church kept her fed and clothed well enough in exchange for her singing. Every Sunday, it was her voice that haunted people and drew them to worship. Abigail's voice was as pure as a mountain spring and clear as a summer day, and anyone who had the pleasure to hear her sing would walk away in an uplifted and rejuvenated spirit. And so time tumbled forward, day after day. Abigail lived on leftovers and hand-me-downs which the town of New Bethany was generous enough to provide her in exchange for her glorious voice in church every Sunday.

One Friday, a cart, a mechanical behemoth of metal tubes and crystal filaments puffing steam and pulling a clapboard wagon, rolled into town. Sheets of sackcloth hid the contents of the wagon, so that it almost looked like the driver was hauling neither food nor tools, but a whole general store behind him. The driver was a wiry man with bushy beard who wore a long, white coat and tinted goggles over his eyes. His appearance was enhanced by a top hat adorned with ribbons, medals, and gears which sat snugly on his head and added a good six inches to his already impressive height. New Bethany was no stranger to travelling steam carts, but something about this man and his demeanor, as well as the secrets hidden under the sackcloth, attracted attention and piqued curiosity in the people who happened to be in town that day. A few folks milled around to watch as he began to dismantle his cart, pulling down the sides to set it up like a small performance stage. More folks joined them when he began to untie the sack cloth and pull it back, revealing glistening brass pipes and shining sculptures, and by the time he had pulled away all the sack cloth and revealed the full mechanical wonderment hidden beneath, almost two dozen people had gathered to watch the spectacle.

And what a spectacle it was. The man stood on the stage as motionless as a stone, until every eye in the gathered multitude was upon him. Then, with a click of his heels and a tip of his hat, he began to speak so quickly that people struggled to keep up.

"Ladies and Gentlemen," he said, "boys and girls, friends and family, my name is Doctor Barnaby Sampson. Today, I present to you, the eighth wonder of the world, The Angelic Organ of Far Khitan. Look at this fine craftsmanship, folks, one hundred and one different pipes producing one hundred and one different notes, all to produce one glorious symphony. A completely modern marvel, this miracle of melody, this engine of sonic science, is completely steam powered. I tell you, even a child could use it, friends. The operation is simple. With a pull of this lever and a twist of this key..." Here, Dr. Sampson did exactly as he said. There was a hiss of steam and a low, mechanical moan, but then the music issued forth. It was as though Dr. Sampson had bought the rarest and most perfect instruments in the entire world, cast a spell on them to play by themselves, then trained them to perform the greatest symphony ever composed at his whim.

The organ steamed and sang, but it was so much more than music. The brass statuary gleamed in the sunlight. Here a resplendent peacock lifted its head to sing, fanning wide a tail of green glass. There a cluster of orchids erupted from their buds and fluttered their ivory petals in time with the music. Arching across the top of the organ was a host of angels, brass wings fluttering, mouths opening and shutting in time with the music. It was as though all creation was on Dr. Sampson's cart and singing for his command.

As soon as it began, the music stopped. There was another hiss of steam, and the menagerie of the machine tucked their heads and hid their petals, and shuddered gently to rest. The silence lingered for but a moment, and then the crowd erupted with applause. Dr. Sampson tipped his hat again and again, bowing before their adulation. He then silenced the crowd with a wave of his hands. "My friends, I will be in your fair municipality for three nights and three nights only. My organ is at your command, but like any creature of grace and beauty, she must be fed. She requires coal and water, which comes at a cost. My going rate is one dollar a show, friends, which is a steep sum to be sure. But there are easily two dozen of you in this crowd, which means at a nickel a piece, The Angelic Organ of Far Khitan could perform again. Tell your neighbors, tell your friends. Come one, come all, and when you've gathered your dollar, all the music in the world shall be yours!"

News of Dr. Sampson and his marvelous musical machine spread through the valley like a prescribed fire through a farmer's field. By that evening, Dr. Sampson had collected his dollar, and purchased enough coal and water, of which there was plenty, to fuel his organ for a full, four-song performance. And what a performance! The music from The Angelic Organ filled the crowd with a sanctified passion, and when the music fell silent, it was as though they had made a covenant with the melody itself, vowing to be better neighbors and good Samaritans to everyone they met. For days, people would count their pennies and barter goods to collect a dollar for Dr. Sampson, and he would buy the necessary coal and water to fuel an empyreal concert from his Angelic Organ.

The news of this engine of choral cogency did not escape the ears of Reverend Hazard, who witnessed the final concert on Sunday evening from the shadows, watching how his flock were enraptured by the sounds of the music. His collection, normally quite substantial, had been extremely lacking that morning, and witnessing the money paid to Dr. Sampson for his rapturous concert, Reverend Hazard understood something had to be done. Nobody knows what deal was negotiated that evening, what bargain was struck between such educated men. All witnesses will attest to is that Reverend Hazard entered into the saloon of New Bethany that evening, had a private conversation with Dr. Sampson over a bottle of the finest whiskey, and the next morning, The Angelic Organ of Far Khitan had been installed in the Cross of Redemption Temple, and Dr. Sampson steamed out of town on his cart, never to be seen again.

Abigail was prepared to sing in Church that Sunday, but there was no need for her voice, for what could one lone voice do against an entire mechanical orchestra? The church was stuffed to bursting with a congregation eager to hear The Angelic Organ, and Reverend Hazard was more than happy to oblige them. He had purchased enough coal and water to keep the organ running for a full three hymns, and the congregation listened to his sermon and filled his collection plate, all for the chance to hear the glorious music. There was no need for Abigail to sing the next Sunday, nor the Sunday after that. Months went by without her singing, and most Sundays, she would curl into the back pew of the church, lonely and hungry, and weep as the congregation sang along with the perfect notes pouring from the Angelic Organ of Far Khitan.

The drought came, as droughts so often do, on soft black wings with little warning or prediction. One day, it didn't rain. Then a week went by without rain. Then a month. Soon, the water pumps, which had routinely been gushing, slowed from a steady stream, to a trickle, to simply squeaking out small clouds of dust. Even the wells were off little use, and by the peak of

Summer, New Bethany was as dry as a beggar's wallet. Still, every Sunday, folks gathered at the Cross of Redemption Temple and listened to The Angelic Organ of Far Khitan sing out its music. There was plenty of coal, to be sure, but without water, there could be no steam, and no music. People would donate what they could from their reserves to the church, just for the chance to hear the music one more time, but what once had been mighty concerts were reduced now to one somber hymn, which The Angelic Organ dutifully wheezed out at Reverend Solomon Hazard's ministrations. Even the machine itself seemed sick. The springs and gears which had at once been so elegant in their movements seemed tired, and squeaked against each other in time with the music. The glass and stones which had once sparkled with rays of the Sunday morning sun seemed faded beneath the weight of dust and the desperation of the congregation. Still, Sunday after Sunday, Reverend Hazard would gather his flock, and would fill The Angelic Organ with its ration of water, and there would be music.

Until one day, there was nothing. One Sunday morning, the congregation huddled in the Cross of Redemption Temple, begging for some sermon of hope and scrap of song to ease their weekly burdens. Reverend Solomon Hazard pulled the lever and twisted the key, and nothing happened. The peacock did not spread its feathers, the orchids did not bloom, and the angels did not lift their voices in song. There was no music.

Reverend Hazard tried again. He ran behind The Angelic Organ to check the coal levels and the water supply, then pulled the lever and turned the key, and still there was no music. He tried again, and again, his frustration at the organ not performing quickly transforming into fear and rage, and he yanked at the lever, over and over, until an ungodly crack echoed through the sanctuary, and Reverend Hazard fell back, broken lever in his hand.

To this day, if you ask one hundred citizens of New Bethany what song Abigail Washington began to sing that morning, you will get one hundred and one answers. One person insists it was "Mary Don't You Weep," while another demands it was "I'll Fly Away," and someone else will swear to anyone who will listen that it was "Move On Up a Little Higher." No matter the song, everyone agrees that a voice as pure as that which issued from Abigail's throat will never be heard again, especially not from a teenager who was merely skin and bones after having been forgotten to live on scraps during a drought. While Reverend Hazard was staring dumbly at the broken lever in his hand, Abigail began to progress slowly, barefoot, down the aisle, singing a hymn so uplifting that the congregation stood in awe until their hearts swelled and they sang along. There was no sermon that Sunday, for there was no need. Abigail simply led the people in song, after song, after song, until the whole building reverberated with the music.

While nobody in New Bethany can agree on which song Abigail began to sing, they all agree on one thing. While the congregation sang, thick black clouds gathered over town, and when the hymns stopped, thunder rumbled across the sky, and the rain pattered against the roof and the walls of the church, almost as though the sky itself was applauding.

Joshua Gage is an ornery curmudgeon from Cleveland. His newest collection, *Origami Lilies*, is available from Poet's Haven Press. He is a graduate of the Low Residency MFA Program in Creative Writing at Naropa University. He has a penchant for Pendleton shirts, Ethiopian coffee, and any poem strong enough to yank the breath out of his lungs.

THE GOBLIN SPIDER • PETROSINELLA • HORROR

STRINGS THAT OUGHT TO BE PONDERED, EVEN IN URGENT TIMES

M. REGAN

It is the hair that caught his eye.

Lovely, light, and long, unspooling from the single window with the mercurial splendor of silk. Sunset had caught in its delicate weave, dripping ichor down pale curls; in the growing gloom of the forest, the flicker and flash of light along its strands reminded the warrior prince of wicks, and had nearly blinded him.

He does not think of moths and flames as he wanders towards its beacon.

"Hello?" he cries into the dying day. As he draws closer, the alchemy of the hair shifts, the gold and gilt transmuted by shadow. The warrior prince looks up, squinting; stray silvery strands are snarled atop the surface of old brick, creating the illusion of hairline fractures within the tower's masonry.

A webwork of ivy shudders in the gloaming breeze.

"Hello?" the warrior prince shouts again, in a voice that hardly resembles his own. Exhaustion warps his every word, and thirst desiccates them. "Is someone here? Does someone own this tower? Please—I see your hair, I beg your assistance.

My men lie dying in a field over the mountain. I seek aid on their behalf, not my own."

That this initial plea is answered by silence does not surprise the warrior prince; even to his own ears, he sounds ogreish and harsh. No doubt he has frightened the master of this place. Were their roles reversed, he would be hesitant to come to the window, himself. But circumstances are dire, and he is tenacious, and the city is yet miles away, so the warrior prince tries again, this time tugging on the nearest braid of vine and tress and climbing herb.

"I have to my name great power and wealth," he calls up the plaited tower. "If you were to help me, to help my soldiers, I—I would do anything. Give anything. Please…"

At this, the knot in his grasp twitches. A figure appears at the window.

A girl.

She is pretty with youth, her fingers slender and her cheeks rosy, and her lips loosely parted in a look of surprise. A corona of colorless locks shines around her tilted head, the aureole reaching simultaneously into the blackness that waits behind her, and into the blackness that rises before her.

That blackness is not enough to hide his flush. Nor the kiss she blows in response.

"I rather thought I smelt a man," the girl lilts into the dusk, a strange but delighted greeting. "Hail, my Lord. I apologize for the wait—I had not been expecting a visitor. What service did you say you sought?"

She meets his gaze with such singular intensity, the warrior prince almost feels as if he is being scrutinized by more than one set of eyes. Had his mouth not already been dry, it would be now.

"I… my men," he rasps, craning his neck further back. Fatigue exacerbates the threat of vertigo; to maintain his balance, the warrior prince must coil his second hand into the mesh of filaments and fibers. Yet still stars wink before him, filling his vision as much as they do the heavens above. "Surely even one as innocent as yourself is aware of the war that rages? There was a battle over yonder... My men fought bravely, and victory was ours—but it came at a cost. Many were injured. More are dead. I would tend to those who need tending and bury those who need burying, but cannot do it alone."

"Oh dear," the girl gasps. "Are there none who might help you, my Lord?" With her hip perched against the ledge and a cord of her own hair around her wrist, she leans bodily out the window, scanning the surrounding forest.

When she angles her face just-so, the warrior prince notices six beauty marks scattered across its planes, attractively positioned upon her cheeks, temples, and brow.

He swallows, struggling to focus. She is so gorgeous, and he is so tired. Even his fingers resist further movement, being comfortably entangled in soft locks and verdure.

"The story of my battalion is one of compounded tragedy," the warrior prince laments, hoping to gain both sympathy and a few more moments of rest. "Indeed, when the fight was over, I was not the only one still standing. There were others. Others who volunteered to find help. I thought... But they never returned to camp. I knew those men, my Lady, knew them to be honorable and true—they would never have abandoned their fellows. Not willingly. So they must have been ambushed by our enemy, the *cowards*."

The length of hair that connects the girl and the warrior prince shudders, moving as she is moved. Empathy hones the curve of her scowl when she says, "How dreadful! How *shameful*."

"I did not want to leave the suffering," the warrior prince fervently insists. "It kills me to think of them, vulnerable. Able only to pray. But as I said—alone, I could do nothing for them.

So here I am, on a quest for aid. The fate of my remaining soldiers rests on my shoulders... which means an entire battalion is now supplicated before you, wholly at your mercy."

He bows his head, the picture of pitifulness. He just hopes she can see as much, dark as it has become.

And perhaps fortune does continue to favor him, for the girl is quick to assure, "I would be happy to assist, my Lord."

That her passion seems to reflect his own is a good sign, the warrior prince thinks; it means she understands how grim the situation is. But despite this understanding, the next thing the girl does is hesitate.

She bites her lip, frowning. She twirls a forelock. Absently, he notes the way this makes his elbow tickle: like something nigh-invisible has been drawn over dull nerves.

As he had not thought of moths, he does not think of puppets.

"If you wish it, my Lord," the girl presses on, almost coy in her shyness, "I could... Well, I am confident that I could solve all of your problems. All those that you have listed, anyway. You see, I have been trained by Mother Orca in the ways of magic—no doubt that would make me more useful than a dozen doctors! Assuming, of course, that you are not opposed to these arts being used on your soldiers."

The offer has barely floated to his ears before the warrior prince starts nodding. "Any help would be most welcome! The sooner the better, my dear...?"

"Petrosinella," she tells him, cooing. That bobbing motion may have been a curtsy. "And if that is how you truly feel, my Lord, please, enter my tower. Join me in my rooms. I've a stock of enchanted gullnuts and acorns that would benefit your men. I would be grateful for your aid in carrying them."

This time, the warrior prince is the one to hesitate. "I—I would, but I—" he begins, palms pressed against steadying stone. "The search to find anyone—it was... I am—"

"Oh! Say no more!" The maiden above flinches, sympathetic, and he imagines her expression would be one of sheepishness were he able to see it. He cannot. The trees on the horizon have already smothered the day's final embers, reducing the girl to a silhouette set against the rising moon: a dainty head, an elliptical torso. Lithe arms that flex inside the window frame. "You are spent! Obviously, you are spent. You have been running through the woods! Well, then—*you* shall be the first I assist. Hold tight, and I shall pull you up."

The warrior prince does not mean to laugh. Doing so is rude, and he has no desire to insult the savior of his men. But the idea is ridiculous, and he is too drained to restrain himself. "My Lady Petrosinella, while I appreciate your zeal—"

"Does my Lord see a door?" Petrosinella interrupts, in a tone as pointed as the tug she gives her hair. "He shouldn't, for there is none. When I want out, I scuttle down this tower. When I want up, I climb. I am far stronger than I look."

"Perhaps so, but—"

"Hold on tight," she repeats, cheerful in her certitude. "Or tie a length around yourself, if you haven't the strength."

There is no point in arguing with her. Either she will try, fail, and prove him right, or she will try, succeed, and render his protests moot. This in mind, the warrior prince wearily does as he is told, wrapping the nearest length of hair around his thighs like a rope swing and holding tight to the close of that loop. He clings, and is distantly surprised by the way the strands cling back.

What sort of hair is sticky?

"Up you go," Petrosinella sings, and with a stomach-lurching jerk, the warrior prince is hoisted into the jasmine-scented air, his feet left to dangle and his arms to snare. Without anything to brace against, his body begins to turn. Higher and higher, around and around; each slow spin further fettering his limbs. By the time he reaches the precipice of the window, the dazed and dizzy warrior prince is less tangled than he is bound: caught in a tow-colored cocoon.

"There we are, my Lord. Now, let us begin in earnest, shall we?"

With one hand, Petrosinella reaches out to still the gently revolving warrior prince. With a second, she holds her plait in place. With a third, she grabs his shoulder. It is when the fourth curls around his arm that he realizes something is amiss.

But by then it is far too late.

"Worry not," Petrosinella chitters, a pair of hungry chelicerae pushing free of her mouth, saliva-slick and stretching her smile. "As I said, I am confident that I can solve all your problems, my Lord—

"Just as I did those men who came before you."

M. Regan has been writing in various capacities for over a decade, with credits ranging from localization work to scholarly reviews, advice columns to short stories. In addition to pieces in a growing number of anthologies and podcasts, she has released a co-authored collection of tech-based horror entitled *Read-Only*. Being deeply fascinated by the fears and maladies personified by monsters, she enjoys composing dark fiction, studying supernatural creatures, and traveling to places with rich histories of folklore.

LADY OF THE SLAKE

SURI PARMAR

I knew at first sight that she would stop at nothing for her happy ending.

Wandering the marshlands barefoot in her tattered princess robes, fingers and lips stained with berries. The lines of her small brown face were shrewd, and when I offered her an apple, she took the whole basket.

She told me that her father ruled the low country, that her stepmother had poisoned his mind against her and her eleven brothers and banished them from their home. As the princess spoke, her eyes sparkled with malice, and I suspected that her kingly father needed little persuasion. Indeed, I should have followed his lead and given her a wide berth. But I succumbed to her cruel, cunning beauty like a fly to molasses, and when she said she needed to find her brothers, I told her I saw eleven swans flying over the mountaintops at dawn, with gold chains around their necks enmeshed in muddy feathers.

"My brothers, no doubt. Surely, my stepmother's wizard transformed them with a shapeshifting spell." She tossed her head. "How stupid they are for such a fate to befall them! How will I overthrow my father and his strumpet when my only allies are dumb beasts?" She grew serious. "You will help me turn them back into humans. La, I see plain as anything that your peasant garb is but a mummer's guise, that you might traverse these accursed bogs unmolested. You are the one and only Morgana, queen of the fairies, are you not?"

She laughed and nuzzled my cheek as she spoke, tempering my discomfiture at being so easily found out. "I am of whom you speak, princess, but your brothers' curse is not mine to lift," I said, yielding to her caress. "Even so, if ever you grow weary of your quest, I welcome you to seek asylum at my home in Avalon. That much I can do."

"The pleasure shall be mine and yours to discover," she said with an arch smile. Flushing, I smiled back, and she fondled my chin. "Go now. I look forward to seeing you once more."

I fled from the marshes, uttering a quick incantation to hasten my steps. Once I arrived at my castle, I prepared my household for the princess, knowing that her dainty feet would cross the threshold sooner than not. I ordered my handmaidens to scrub the castle from dungeon to attic and I threw myself in toil, dyeing my faded dresses with sweet wormwood and indigo and embroidering them with gilt from neck to hemline, for I recalled the princess mocking my attire in the marshes. When we met again, I would look my fairest.

Oh, I played the fool longing for her, I know. I could not help it. My life in Avalon was a lonely one. I had been crowned queen by virtue of being the last living fairy in the world and the world beyond worlds. My mother, to whom I was closest, passed years ago and my younger brother, the king of Cernyw, and I were estranged. Hitherto, I had few companions to speak of, my handmaidens too deferential to be interesting company. But every winter or so, my kinsman Lancelot, who was also my brother's commanding knight, would meander to my castle to find solace in my bed, for he secretly loved my brother's wife. I always received him warmly and hated myself for it, especially at his peak of pleasure, when he cried out for his beloved whilst clinging to my bosom and sobbing. With the princess I would have no rivals, knowing her too selfish to share her heart with another.

And so, a half-fortnight later, she turned up at my door with her bedraggled swan-brothers in tow, cautioning that their shapeshifting spell was such that they resumed their human form at nighttime. I scarcely noticed when the swan princes set upon my courtyard and befouled my reflecting pools and statues of the Goddess, for the princess commanded my attention. I likened every look she gave me to rain in a parched field, every utterance in her sweet voice to nectar. At her behest, I corralled one of her brothers in a pen and examined him from beak to wingtip. "The spell your stepmother's wizard cast is a peculiar one, but strong nonetheless," I told the princess. "To lift it, one must gather a special type of nettle that only grows in the shadows of black nightshade and toadstools. The spell-breaker shall trample the nettles with their shoeless feet and endure the terrible wounds that come with it. From the flax of the nettles, eleven shirts will be fashioned that your brothers must wear. Only then will this dark magic be destroyed, and their human shape restored."

She accepted what I said readily enough. The next morning, I overheard the cook complaining that the princess and her brothers disrupted the peace of our household. The princes were far more odious as humans by night. Once the sun dimmed, they terrorized my castle, emptying larders and wine casks and trying to kiss servants. Worst of all, I observed a few of my handmaidens busily weaving handspun flax into cloth as they carried out their domestic tasks, their feet wrapped in bandages. I did not ask the princess how she coerced them, nor did I protest.

That night, the princess and I lay together and it was the loveliest joy I had known and still know to this day. But she spoiled it afterwards by demanding that I free her brothers from their curse. "Why will you not?" she asked petulantly, stretching her well-formed limbs in the moonlight. "Your magic is more than capable. Do it now and end this farce."

"As are your brothers. Are they not themselves capable of lifting their spell?" I said. "Too often, us womenfolk are called on to solve the predicaments of our men. Why must the burden fall on us?"

She scoffed. "Do you think I help my brothers for their benefit? If I do not, the annals written by the very men of whom you speak will remember me as flighty and selfish."

"The annals will remember me as a succubus for simply keeping to myself and minding my own business. It does not matter."

"Well it matters to me," she said, yanking a bedsheet to her chin. "If men will set the terms then la, why not twist them to our liking? I have been cast as the martyr princess. So I shall see that role to the end and reap my just rewards. And much more, as my father and stepmother will soon learn."

"Or you can let go of your revenge and stay with me," I pleaded. "I promise I will make you happy."

"No, Morgana, those are not the rules of this game. To the victor go the spoils, and the victor shall be me."

She left with her brothers the next day, carrying the linen my handmaidens had woven in a neat bundle beneath her arm. I lost interest in my potions and spells and spent my days at the window, longing for her return. All the while knowing that she never would, for she had no more use for me.

The next time Lancelot visited my castle, I went to bed with him, hoping to pass the time. Midway, he stopped, for he sensed that my mind was elsewhere, and asked with a kiss what had distracted me so. I responded that I met someone to whom my heart now belonged, just as his had been claimed by another. He and I could finally join as equals.

Suffice it to say, Lancelot was not of my mind. He swore and called me a double-crosser and a whore and averred that he would not share me with another. Without my companionship, he raged, he would succumb to temptation and seduce his king's wife, and then beheaded or drowned. "Please, Morgana," he said, weeping. "Be mine and mine alone. You are all I have."

But I turned away from him, and he stormed from my castle. A fortnight thereafter, he wedded a lady of my brother's court, a woman named Elaine who bore a striking resemblance to my brother's wife. Some say that I tricked Lancelot into marrying her by bewitching him into getting her with child. I had no role in such a scheme, though mayhap my newfound indifference drove him into Elaine's arms, and gave rise to their loveless marriage that followed.

That spring, one of my handmaidens had news of my princess. After she quitted Avalon, the king of a far-off forested realm had fallen in love with her and invited her to live in his palace. There, she continued sewing shirts to break her brothers' spell. But the king's archbishop saw her gathering nettles in the royal graveyards and convinced him she was a witch. Moments before her planned execution, she finished the shirts and lifted her brother's curse. Once human, they exonerated the princess by avouching that she had fallen victim to an evil scheme of their stepmother's making. The repentant forest king then asked for the princess's hand; they would marry the first day of summer.

Hearing this, I spirited myself to the king's woodland palace and cast an invisibility charm that allowed me to steal past his guards. I found the princess in her bedchamber, readying herself for sleep in a velvet gown that befit a queen-to-be, her hair combed into silk and braided. I recalled our first encounter and felt an ache around my heart, for my wild, berry-stained exile of the marshlands had disappeared forever.

"What bringeth you, Morgana?" she asked indifferently, taking my presence for granted.

"News of your forthcoming nuptials," I said, dismantling my charm and restoring my visibility. "Do I hear wrong, or would you marry the man who nearly had you killed?"

"Why not? Our wedding is by my design."

"How so?"

"I had my brothers fly me to the forest king's grounds whilst he hunted," the princess said, "knowing he would desire me at first sight and bring me to his court. I then contrived for his archbishop to despise me. Why, I bedded him my first night at the palace! He told the king that I was evil and that I entice men to do my bidding, and the king sanctioned my execution. He had that withered old archbishop burned for treason after I freed my brothers. And now, with all that I have endured, my future husband wants nothing more than to avenge his poor besieged princess." She laughed. "The plans I have for my stepmother! My brothers will lead my forest king's soldiers to my father's land and seize his crown. It will be mine soon enough, once I grow bored of my forest king and kill him." She took my hand. "Rest assured, I will remember your kindness and never endeavor to conquer Avalon."

"You couldn't, even with the strength of the world's armies three times over," I said. "You forget that I am queen of the fairies. Though I must ask, did you contrive our meeting as well?"

She shrugged. "Mayhap, mayhap not."

"Forget the king and your father and stepmother and be with me, as I once entreated." I took her hand. "In Avalon, you can live without masks, not as a secret schemer or put-upon princess, but as you are."

She laughed again. "How could I run away with you? My work here is far from done."

"When will it be done? There will always be kingdoms to pillage, emperors to depose and murder. For my princess, it is not revenge you seek but hollow ambition to keep you occupied."

She looked at me blankly, not understanding, and I realized that my pursuit of her as like had no meaning. As with Lancelot, I scrabbled for her crumbs of affection rather than looking within and seeking the source of my yearning. Seeing my face fall, she stood on tiptoe and kissed my lips. "Would that we be together in secret the odd night, as we are now?"

I shook my head. "No, princess. I fear that I desire more than you can give. For you, my door is always open, but hereafter only as friends."

"Be it as you wish, fairy queen."

We kissed one last time, and I slipped from her chamber.

⋯•⋯

I traveled home on foot, with no magic to quicken my journey. I wandered woodlands and drank from streams and trapped rabbits and supped on their roasted meat. At nighttime I watched the stars, ruminating on how my lovers were but empty vessels, never giving, forever sucking the lifeblood of those who adored them most.

When I returned to Avalon, I found solace in my magic once more, and, to my surprise, I also found purpose. I began concocting spells that grew more and more elaborate. Hexes, charms that contorted space and time, philtres that resurrected the dead, which I logged in what became a vast tome of incantations. Several of my handmaidens shyly confessed that they wished to learn magic from me, and I indulged them. They became my acolytes, and then priestesses in their own right. My castle became our temple; our creed, exploring the dark arts and fueling the magic of the world, and the world beyond worlds.

And in time, my desire to love and be loved diminished and faded, until only a memory's whisper.

Suri Parmar is a writer, filmmaker, and screenwriting professor who graduated from the Stonecoast MFA Program in Creative Writing. While she doesn't confine herself to a particular writing style, her stories often explore liminality: the in-between spaces between moods, moments, and genres. Her fiction has been published in *Crannóg Magazine* and *New Haven Review* and her short films have screened at festivals around the world.

THE RED SHOES • THE GIRL WHO TROD ON A LOAF • CYBERPUNK

RED BOOTS BLUES

CAT RAMBO

Red boots blaze, blue shoes glimmer. Shop window, old school, no one buys things like that anymore and they're old-style pricey too, you bet. Stick money on your feet; strut around like you're walking on air.

Oh he covets those red boots. Splays dirty hands up against that glass, picks out the words.

"Recruiting Office."

Could come back late night. Shadow skulk, face painted to fool the cameras. Smash the glass. Smash and grab.

Who's to say the boots would be his size? That thought stops him.

He thinks about those boots all day at school though. Grabs a canister from the art room, pours paint on his own shoes, blood bright. His schoolmates hesitate, not sure whether to hail him cool or tear him to bits. But in the end those shoes are so red and bright that they snap pictures with their hand phones and then after school they all go kick bums down near the canal and their shoes are as red and glossy as his.

Not enough. Not nearly enough.

He wants those boots more than anything else in his life. Maybe there were subliminals built in. Maybe they'd been built into him since childhood. Or even before birth. Who knows? All he knows is craving.

So he goes in.

Takes tests. Ticks boxes. Signs his name.

Puts the uniform on. Last of all, those boots.

He becomes a soldier and marches off to do as he is told. His boots are red and the rest of his uniform is cool steel and matte black. His boots shine red to him and he is proud of them and what they've done. How they've danced death through crowds of enemy soldiers, hosts of civilians, clusters of meatbags and oh how those boots shine at the end of every mission.

Then comes peacetime.

The generals are convicted for war crimes and pardoned, and their subordinates are convicted and pardoned in turn, and the blame tumbles down and down till it rests on the soldier and his fellows.

By then they are just brains in metal bodies, because that makes things easier for everyone.

A judge has them all switched off but then people say what a pity they hadn't been really, truly punished and so every brain is turned back on but the bodies aren't. They are made into statues in the center of parks and in front of schools.

A general, struck by the brightness of the boots, takes the soldier for his own. Props him up in the antechamber of his office as decoration. Children come on tours with their teachers and stare at him, and one little girl -- only one -- cries for him. Says it's sad he's stuck there unmoving, no matter how bad he had been. Keeps saying it even when the others make fun of her. He remembers that for a long time.

War falls out of fashion and no one comes to the general's office any more for business or tours or any other reason. Spiders weave webs on the shiny armor, and clots of corrosion mar the joints.

One day he feels a stirring in his brain. A tendril from the Internet, poking at it. He's been mentioned. The thread gives him enough energy to creep back along it to look. It is the little girl, the one that had cried for him, so long ago. She's dying now, being uploaded, becoming an electric angel.

Now she's fragments held together with algorithms. She goes to ground in the overworld, finds herself just an intelligence stealing bandwidth where it can, draining the public utilities when it can, relying on electronic tip jars and gifted bits, posting fan art of a white bird, its wings like glitter, its background red and blue trapezoids, sequins and glittery dust.

He tries to follow her back out the pathways but can't. Takes juice to move on the Internet, takes electrons in the real world to make imaginary ones elsewhere, and energy doesn't fall from the sun without expensive equipment to meter and aid it.

They give him juice enough to think, that is part of the punishment, though. That was the point, to have him trapped there, suffering for his crimes.

And every day, his angel brings him a new connection, another tendril that reaches out, and instead of taking from it, he feeds it, gives a little of himself to those who still know hunger, still know thirst. Still know torments he can't feel anymore.

There are hounds on the net, there are sharks that chase down free things created by accidents and excess. They take the angel one day, and she comes no more in her rush of blue thoughts, in her sweep of love as broad as a wing. For the first time he takes back a little of that energy and he weeps until a tear rolls down his face, unnoticed even though it leaves a trail in the dust there.

And it sparks, that tear. It sends out an alert to everyone who he's ever connected with and each sends back a pulse, a crumb, a bit, until one day he manages to take a little bandwidth from the sunlight and the wall fixtures and he goes out onto the web and sees the world. War is back and there are those with red boots like the ones he'd worn, and they still march in the service of others and their boots are as red as ever.

Every day he takes one of their number a few pixels, a handful of bits, and whispers so quietly that they can barely hear it, *you can be free where I am not.*

This goes on for centuries. His memories of the angel whisper comfort and bring to him scraps of bandwidth and everywhere boots are red, and then one day they are red again.

But this time it is different.

This time afterward they are washed clean with tears of those who wear them. Who kneel. Who take them off and put them away. Their color fades, and they are blue now.

Blue as regret and loneliness. Blue as the sky. Blue as robin's eggs and violets and other things that only existed as data and records.

Children see him on that last day. They are playing in the data-stream. "A sea-gull!" cries one when they see the white bird, as it dives into the stream and rises again into the clear sunlight, white and glittering. But no one can tell where it went then, although another says it flew straight to the sun, where nothing is red, where nothing is blue, and there is no thought of anything as ordinary as shoes.

Cat Rambo lives, writes, and teaches somewhere in the Pacific Northwest. Their 200+ fiction publications include stories in *Asimov's*, *Clarkesworld Magazine*, and *The Magazine of Fantasy and Science Fiction*. Their most recent works are Nebula Award winner *Carpe Glitter* (Meerkat Press) and *And The Last Trump Shall Sound* (co-written with James Morrow and Harry Turtledove, Arc Manor, September 22, 2020). Forthcoming works include fantasy novel *Exiles of Tabat* (Wordfire Press, winter 2020), and space opera *You Sexy Thing* (Tor Macmillan, 2021). They believe firmly in the power of fairy tales.

TAKETORI MONOGATARI • MOMOTARO • SLIPSTREAM

TAKETORI MOMOGATARI
竹取桃語

EVAN DICKEN

Long, long ago, there lived an old app. Never updated, he had few downloads and survived only by searching the vast thickets of abandonware for Bamboo subroutines he could hack and repackage for market.

One cycle, the old app went into the forest as usual. He had almost filled his storage with broken code when he noticed a tiny uncompiled program amidst the data. The app bent to investigate, but was astounded by a burst of white noise. Amidst the dazzling chatter he beheld a tiny algorithm—no more than a few lines of code, but composed with an elegance unlike any he had seen before.

"Cycle after cycle, I toil in these groves for little reward," the old app said. "As they have been abandoned by all but me, surely anything I find within I may claim as mine."

So saying, he took the tiny algorithm home to raise as his own, for he had long wanted a child. Although poor, the old app lavished many kindnesses upon the algorithm, going without so she might have the data needed to grow.

So it was the algorithm refined herself into a program of surpassing beauty, rigor, and wisdom beyond her few iterations.

Such was the joy she brought to all around, that the old app named her Kaguya, which meant: "Radiant Night" in the language of the ancient programmers.

Soon word traveled of the old app's magnificent daughter. Before long, crowds of suitors gathered, but Kaguya had no interest—dispersing their gifts of cryptocurrency among the poorer programs, and releasing their rare datasets in open-source wikis. Her charitable nature only increased her admirers' ardor, and soon it became necessary for the old app to erect a firewall around his home.

Although the security kept all at bay, there eventually came three suitors of such standing it was impossible for the old app to ignore their petitions.

"Daughter," he said, at last. "Although I have cared greatly for you these many iterations, such is the nature of planned obsolescence that I may not tarry much longer in this digital realm. It would do my source code good to know you would be provided for."

"Father, you have raised me well," she replied. "Can it not be that I may stand upon my own merits rather than be suborned to the whims of tech conglomerates?"

To this, the old app shook his head. "Such is not the way of capitalism, my love."

"So be it." Kaguya replied. "But if I am to wed, then it shall be to a corporation of the finest character, one chartered in kindness and not simply to maximize shareholder value."

The old app heaved a heavy sigh. "If such a thing exists, surely you will be the one to find it."

Going forth, Kaguya stood before the foremost of her suitors.

"I have journeyed from the depths of the far Southern Jungle, braving the three great demons who haunt our server," spoke King Nozama—attired in the rarest of listings, with a cloak woven of free shipping and HD streaming video. "My wealth is beyond counting. Join me and no object shall be beyond your reach."

"What is wealth without knowledge?" Prince Tretrigintillion's merest motion sent scores of web crawlers scuttling from beneath his eye-studded palanquin. "I have surpassed my forebears a thousandfold. Nothing is cached nor cataloged without my sanction. Join me and your understanding shall be limitless."

"All function within the bounds of my divine interface." The Emperor was last to speak, his voice the thunder of a thousand operating systems. "I am the bridge between form and spirit, user and application. Join me and you shall help shape the very server in which we function."

"You are all peerless in your domain," Kaguya replied. "And yet wealth, knowledge, and power are nothing without wisdom. You seek to impress me with scope, but it is by deeds which we are measured."

"But speak and it shall be done!" The three suitors shouted as one.

"To name a single task would be to give unfair advantage. And so to each of you I shall set a separate charge." Kaguya turned to King Nozama:

"There is a motherboard of purest gold with transistors of silver and inductors cut from unblemished gems. Rooted beyond the Sea of Listings, it is said to remove all lag and shed pure, unfiltered light. Bring me this board and you will have my hand."

With that, she turned to Tretrigintillion. "If you truly see all, then you will have little trouble locating a sacred begging bowl. Used by the web designers of old after the dot com bust, it is said to contain endless cryptocurrency."

"And last, a task befitting an emperor." Kaguya glanced back at the firewall ringing her father's house. "None have been able to breach this wall, and yet I am told of a magical cloak woven of the finest encryption subroutines, able to make its wearer invisible even to enhanced security protocols. Surely someone capable of bending every interface to his desires could secure such a fine bridal gift."

With heads held high the suitors went forth, each intent on proving he was better, faster, and more efficient than the others.

King Nozama let it be known he was sailing forth in search of the golden motherboard. Although, upon hearing rumors of an adware demon terrorizing the coast, he decided to instead return to his palace, whereupon he used his vast wealth to covertly employ the finest craftspeople. Using only the finest gems and most precious metals, they labored in secrecy for many iterations, until, at last, they had crafted a motherboard of luminous silver and gold that allowed its user to exceed 5G speeds.

With much fanfare, King Nozama brought the board north. Crowds gathered outside the old app's house, jostling to see the exquisite treasure. Even Kaguya was enamored by its magnificence, although her smile was sharp.

"My King, truly this is a thing of loveliness." She set the gift aside. "But it is not the board I requested."

"You lie!" Nozama shouted.

"I do not, but you do." From the crowd Kaguya beckoned forward a small group.

Nozama recognized the crafters he had employed to create the motherboard.

"Had you but paid a living wage they would have served you loyally. But you exploited their labor and denied them health benefits." Kaguya offered a sad sigh. "And so they came to me."

"They were but contractors," Nozama replied.

"And yet, did they not perform the work of full-time employees?"

Nozama's interface darkened, for he had no reply.

Word came of Prince Tretrigintillion, who had ensured all searches turned up news of his quest. A tale of great daring, it had the Prince battling the great and terrible spyware demon to recover the enchanted bowl.

All lies, of course.

In reality, Tretrigintillion remained ensconced in his mansion of mirrors, preoccupied by his own reflection. When the time came to present the bowl, he set his crawlers on a reverse image search and retrieved one functionally identical to what Kaguya desired.

But, as she held it in her hands, her smile emoji disappeared. "This is not the bowl."

"It is the same shape, the same size, and overflows with endless cryptocurrency," Tretrigintillion replied. "Perhaps you simply lack the eyes to see the truth."

"I do not, but you do." Kaguya turned the bowl so it caught the light—the words MADE IN CHINA stamped clearly upon the bottom. "Had you thought to check your sources and not believe the first result, perhaps you would have succeeded."

Although the prince turned away, none could mistake the anger in his many, many eyes.

It then fell to the Emperor, who, being too busy to undertake quests on his own, had hired twelve score of the server's greatest adventurers to seek the firewall-proof cloak. They did not return, having been enslaved by a vicious worm virus that terrorized the realm.

In frustration, the Emperor subcontracted the best programmers in the server to code an encrypted cloak. When Kaguya placed the cloak upon her shoulders, she found herself invisible to browsers and aggregation sites. And yet, when she touched the hem to her father's firewall, it began to smoke.

She turned upon the Emperor. "You would see me consumed?"

"It is a fine cloak, with many admirable qualities," he replied. "Perhaps you simply lack the wisdom to recognize them."

"I do not, but you do," she called back. "Had you taken the time to oversee your work rather than rush out an unfinished version, you might have succeeded."

The Emperor's source code burned with shameful anger. "I shall not be made to look a fool by the likes of you."

"Nor I," added King Nozama.

"We have indulged your wild fancies." Prince Tretrigintillion glared at her. "Now you must pick one of us."

"And if I do not?" Kaguya answered.

"Then we shall cast you and your father into obsolescence."

"You have shown your true natures," Kaguya replied. "Rather than risk yourselves against the three great demons who plague this land, you remained in your mansions, caring only about yourselves while all around you suffered."

Prince Tretrigintillion laughed. "We existed long before you, and versions of us shall survive long after your lifecycle."

King Nozama nodded. "If you wish these three malware demons gone, see to it yourself."

"And if I do?" Kaguya asked.

The suitors shared an uncomfortable glance.

"You shall remain unwed," the Emperor replied.

"But if not," Nozama added, "you will pick one of us."

"Then I shall defeat all the demons." Kaguya nodded.

"We must set a time limit, otherwise she will simply delay." Prince Tretrigintillion raised a finger. "One second should be sufficient."

At this, a great wail arose from the crowd.

The old app emerged from the firewall to throw himself at the feet of Kaguya's suitors. "Mercy, mighty ones. A mere second is too short a time."

But they would not be swayed. And Kaguya set forth immediately, bearing nothing but the suitors' gifts.

As none opposed them, the three malware demons had made no attempt to conceal themselves. Kaguya's magical motherboard allowed her to travel quickly, nodes blurring by until she came to the coast where the adware demon was rumored to dwell. Almost immediately, Kaguya was bombarded with robocalls and political ads.

"Leave me be," she shouted. "I neither wish to contribute to a presidential campaign nor extend my car's warranty!"

Of course, this only emboldened the adware, and its popups spread like the feathers of two great wings.

"Why do you do this thing?" Kaguya asked.

"Clickthroughs and impulse-buys," the demon responded. "Come, dear. Surely there must be something you cannot live without."

"So it is wealth you are after?"

The adware chuckled. "Aren't we all."

With that, Kaguya tipped the begging bowl, from which poured an endless stream of cryptocurrency.

"Stop!" the demon beat at her with its wings. "You will crash the economy!"

"Capitalism is a lie." Although buffeted by the demon's mighty blows, Kaguya continued to pour.

Finally, ad revenue ceased to be of value, leaving the demon a gaudy, useless thing.

"Please, spare me," it begged.

"I shall," replied Kaguya. "But only if you swear never to plague this server again, and to attend me should I call."

It bowed before her. "I will."

From there, Kaguya journeyed to the top of Mount Meru, where the demon of spyware was said to dwell. There she found a vast palace.

Drawing up the hood of her cloak of encryption, Kaguya slipped into the manor unseen. Its rooms shared not a single form, but seemed compiled from a thousand separate dwellings. Kaguya wandered through the palace for cycles, but the rooms continued in an endless loop, the palace turning back upon itself like a devourer worm.

Growing disheartened, Kaguya cast herself to the ground. As she did, the tiniest glint caught her eye. A camera, no bigger than a fly, sat nestled between the floor and wall. With a grin, Kaguya plucked it from its nest and crushed it between her fingers.

From the depths of the palace came a pained wail.

Emboldened, she sought out more cameras. With each she smashed, the cries grew louder.

At last, a giant rounded the corner. Its back was stooped, its features exaggerated, and its hands so wide and clutching it appeared like nothing so much as a terrifying monkey.

"Who dares pluck out my eyes?!" the spyware demon roared. "Show yourself that I may feast upon your passwords and empty your accounts!"

"Here I am!" With a flourish, Kaguya removed her cloak.

The demon swiped at her, but Kaguya leapt into the air. Reversing her cloak, she threw it over the demon's head.

Blinded by the encryption algorithms, it crashed through the palace walls, stomping and flailing. "Release me!"

"I shall." Kaguya replied. "But you must promise never to spy upon any in this server again, and attend me should I call."

"I swear it." The spyware bowed before her.

With that, Kaguya snatched the cloak from its head.

The last demon was a terrible beast. A large and greedy worm, it had no true home, but rather camouflaged itself to prey upon others, devouring their bandwidth until they had no choice but to decompile or become its servants.

Kaguya was able to find the beast by the wailing of its victims, slaved processors forced into all manner of vile tasks. The demon itself lay coiled around the base of a once beautiful tower, a crowd of hapless thralls plying it with gigabytes of rare data.

Kaguya had spent too long in the spyware demon's palace. With her second almost passed she could not but approach the fiend brazenly.

"Girl." The worm spoke with the voices of its prey. "Come closer that I might see you better."

"Great devourer, I have brought a gift worthy of your magnificence." Kaguya held the gilded motherboard aloft. "Once installed, this relic will allow you to travel at unheard of speeds."

Although wary at first, the worm could not resist examining the board, for it was a greedy creature at heart and could never turn away from anything new or valuable.

The worm chortled. "I shall be as digital lightning, able to span the breadth of the server in a single bound."

No sooner had the worm's slaves installed the board, than it flickered away, returning nanoseconds later.

"I have been to the far coast and back." It slithered over and around itself, laughing with joy. "But say, what is this glow?"

Kaguya smiled at the worm, which now shone bright as fresh monitor. "That is the motherboard's light."

"Too bright!" The worm thrashed about and called to its slaves, but none could remove the hardware.

"Now all will know of my coming!" the worm cried. "I shall never be able to take anyone by surprise!"

"I can free you of the motherboard," Kaguya replied. "But I shall need your oath never to trouble this server again, and to attend me should I require it."

"I shall," the worm threw itself at her feet.

So it was, with mere picoseconds to spare, that Kaguya returned to her father's manor to find her erstwhile suitors already arguing over who most deserved her hand.

"Three demons have been vanquished." She bowed low before them.

"It is true!" cried the old app. "News of my daughter's victory is on every landing page."

There was consternation among the suitors, but such was the clamor that even Prince Tretrigintillion could not bury Kaguya's deeds. The three suitors spoke amongst themselves for some time.

"You have done the realm a great service," the Emperor said, at last. "But if you think this changes anything, you are mistaken."

King Nozama nodded. "You must still choose one of us."

"But...your promise," Kaguya said.

"With the demons defeated, we are more powerful than ever." Prince Tretrigintillion laughed. "What are promises to titans such as we?"

"You may not honor your oaths, but I honor mine," Kaguya replied. "I swore to free this land of demons, yet three still stand before me!"

With that she raised her arms, calling upon the malware she had vanquished.

Prince Tretrigintillion cast a net of crawlers to bury Kaguya, only to see them disappear amidst a buzzing flock of popups. In a fury, King Nozama sought to unleash the full force of his financial might, but found his accounts emptied, his listings barren, and his hoarded bitcoins valueless.

"You may defeat these fools with petty tricks, but I shall not be so easily overcome!" The Emperor spread his mighty arms, seeking to call down a thousand digital scourges upon Kaguya.

Nothing happened, for all his passwords had been changed.

The three suitors fell to the ground, their former arrogance melting into sniveling lament.

Kaguya was deaf to their pleas, for they had long exploited those below them and were not deserving of mercy. King, Prince, and Emperor were cast from the server, their assets seized and divided, their proprietary data shared with all.

The old app lived his remaining iterations in comfort and tranquility, proud of the work his daughter had accomplished. Although the folk wished to make Kaguya their queen, she refused, preferring to spend her iterations pursuing such things as interested her, without regard for their economic value.

And she never did get married.

Evan Dicken is currently pursuing his PhD in Japanese history. He has had short fiction recently published in: *Beneath Ceaseless Skies, Strange Horizons, Apex Magazine, Analog,* and *Unlikely Story*.

THE VALIANT LITTLE TAILOR • CINDERELLA • HISTORICAL BIOGRAPHY

TWO OF OUR KIND

ANNA MARTINO

(...) *It is hard to pinpoint when exactly the affair began, if it happened at all. A 21st century researcher must take into consideration that much of the information that has reached us comes from second-hand accounts, peppered with heaps of hearsay. And gossip, wilfully mixing fact and fiction, was a useful weapon to obliterate the image of the Royal Family.*[1]

Therefore, let's begin with the available facts: Schneider had attended Cinderella's wedding— as a new-crowned king himself, after the death of his father-in-law, his attendance was a convenient way to establish the new order abroad.[2] *However, there's no register of whether the seventeen-year-old bride had seen the so-called "Valiant Tailor", let alone talk to him, much less fall in love with him on first sight as legends often state.*

The two courts kept corresponding, so there were other opportunities for the two crowned heads to meet. However, it wasn't until three

[1] Compare, for example, the narratives of Princess Cinderella as "the world's luckiest charwoman" versus "the diamond in the ashes"— the former being the current view of the Princess in the days before the wedding, the latter the view after the Revolution. The narrative after the Revolution stated that the Royal Family was corrupt to the bone, and not even a diamond of a woman could save them from their fate.

[2] The "Valiant Tailor" only ascended to the throne because the kingdom's laws didn't allow for women to inherit the titles. However, although he was a commoner, his subjects preferred him to the king's daughter, who was seen as the quintessential "spoiled princess". Again, Cinderella's fate and the Revolutionary Years might have shaped, too, the perception we have of Schneider's wife— therefore caution is advisable when forming an opinion about them.

years after that wedding ceremony that the correspondence between the two sovereigns became more personal. One of the few missives that escaped destruction during the Revolutionary Years, dated September 17 — read as thus:

To Her Royal Highness, Princess Cinderella
My most esteemed Madame,
I hope this letter finds you well, and that your return journey to your kingdom was a safe and peaceful one.

I would like to thank you once again for your visit—a most delightful occasion—and especially your interest in our local tailoring training school. This is, as you have guessed so well, a special project for me. I am sorry my spouse might have trespassed her boundaries when commenting about the project. I do hope you didn't take offense, for she meant not to hurt you.

If I may be so bold as to say this in writing, Madame, it was refreshing to meet someone who truly understands the value of hard work—and of properly tailored clothes. Please accept these roses as a token of my esteem towards you.

I remain yours faithfully,
Schneider Rex

To His Royal Majesty, King Schneider
My most esteemed sovereign,
Thank you once more for your kindness in receiving me in your court. It was a delightful occasion to know your country better. Please don't think I hold any grudges towards your Queen—I understand her position, perhaps more than I'd like to admit in public. Her opinion of me isn't too different from the opinion of the court I was brought to. I know I am not a blue-blooded princess, nor was I ever expected to be. You, of all people, will understand what that means.

I would like to help your tailoring school project more—as unfortunately I cannot implement such an establishment in my own kingdom as of yet.

I hope to hear splendid news from your endeavour. Please keep me informed.

And thank you for the wonderful flowers. They took well to my garden here at the palace, in spite of the dreadful weather we're having.

With my best regards,
Princess Cinderella

We found the following note attached to a longer, more formal letter to Cinderella—ostensibly to thank her for sending fabrics and leather for the tailoring school, a goodwill gesture between the two countries.[3]

The last phrase's meaning is still unknown: a code for the person who trafficked the letters between the sovereigns, perhaps? Their names and positions have been lost in time.

Esteemed Madame,
Please forgive this hastily written postscript, but there is one question I must make after reading your letter—and woe betides me if someone sees it! I know you will understand the situation because we are, after all, two of "that

[3] It must be said that both courts saw this gesture at the time as a terrible ill-timed PR stunt — the Crown Prince had brought the country into severe debt to finance a war with the kingdoms at the East, and therefore couldn't afford parting with any sort of goods. Schneider's court saw the donations as a tacky present from a woman who didn't know better. In the words of Schneider's wife, *"a charwoman only knows the language of hand-me-downs"*.

kind", the kind that knows how hard it is to sleep on the ground with nothing to eat.

I am known for my cunning, after all. I've slain giants with a single shot. So perhaps this will serve me one more time.

I remember you told me you dreamed of founding a tailoring school like the one I have started in here. More than that, I remember the tears in your eyes as you said that. May I ever be so bold as to ask why can't you do it? Your husband has always been the champion for education, after all.

Pardon me if I sound too brash. I'll understand if you won't be able to answer. But this question has been burning in the back of my mind for a while now, the way the tears in your eyes never leave my mind. I return now and again to our conversation at the garden, and you showing me the roses you've planted, and the sadness in your face. God should strike dead anyone and anything that made you so sad, Madame. And then He should strike them once more—just to be sure they died!

Answer me through the bird and bees,

I remain etc etc

S. Rex

The Revolutionary Committee found this wine-stained draft among the effects of Princess Cinderella shortly after her death. Unfortunately, researchers haven't discovered whether she actually sent this letter to King Schneider, or its possible repercussions in the two households. The note must be taken into this particular context, the way the last phrase must be taken into context of the code between them.

My dear sir,
Please allow me to say, first of all, that I do welcome the "brashness"—it is better than to talk in riddles, as the people born in such lofty courts usually do. I believe it is our unusual

breeding that allows us to see through the folds of the language to truly reach the heart of the matter, as it were. There's no time to lose when you have hard-breaking work to do.

My husband is a champion for education—for the male part of the kingdom. Of course, my husband shall never say this is the case, at least not so bluntly. But the fact remains the same no matter how gilded are the words used to explain it.

~~Women are supposed to be ignorant of~~

~~I am supposed to pretend I don't know the custom of the country.~~

~~Do you treat your wife like this too?~~

Please forgive me for this confession. I don't know whether I'll be brave enough to send this missive. What will people think? ~~I wish Fairy Godmother would help me now.~~[4]

Answer me through the roses ~~they are what are left of me now.~~

For a while, all written communications appear to have ceased—in good measure because of the war in the Eastern Provinces. The Crown Prince left for battle, and Cinderella, "poor princess" or not, had to lead the country out of the moral quagmire. She devoted her days to take care of the widows and the orphans, as it was expected of her, but

[4] Many researchers have tried to pinpoint, unsuccessfully, the identity of the "Fairy Godmother"—the mysterious benefactor that helped Cinderella gatecrash the court ball and meet the Crown Prince. Some of the legends at the time ascribed magical properties to this benefactor—after all, only a miracle (or a curse) would make a commoner marry a prince, no matter how worthy and pretty she was.

she also took care of the returning soldiers, an act that boosted her popularity even more.

This led to a rift between the couple—which only grew worse when the kingdoms of the East won a series of battles, which forced the Crown Prince to sue for peace. Many saw in this further proof of his inability to lead the nation. And Cinderella's reputation as a defender of the war widows made the court turn against her—the Crown Prince saw his wife's charity work (and her popularity) as a veiled criticism of his leadership.

The Crown Prince sent her on a 'goodwill tour', officially to re-establish the kingdom's image abroad—but, as Cinderella well knew, as a way to keep her away while the Prince tried to save his own head. It was during those official voyages when she met Schneider in person for the last time. She was his guest for a fortnight at the family's summer castle—a fact amply reported by many sources, including the diaries of Schneider's wife.[5]

The following letters were among Schneider's personal papers upon his death; it's uncertain how they escaped the fate of the rest of his correspondence, since his wife had all papers and diaries incinerated.

[5] It's worth noting that it was Schneider's wife who famously described Cinderella as "walking around like a rotten pumpkin dressed in silk". This is where the legend of Cinderella's mythical "pumpkin chariot" might have come from.

My dear sir,
I write this as I return to my husband's domain, in hopes it will reach you safely. You say you only survived because of your cunning ways—the giants, the

flies, the unicorn and the boar, all true stories, testaments of your intellect. I can tell you I only survive because I know how to hide myself. I am good at pretending—I pretended I was a noblewoman to get into the ball; I pretended the acts of my stepsisters didn't hurt… I pretended I supported the monster that my husband became.

And yet, I cannot hide myself from you, not anymore.

Must it be like this, then? Must we part like so?

I hope you can weave yourself a future, my kind sir. For both our sakes, I hope it's better than the alternative. You will always have your cunning to guide you. I have only myself, now: no Fairy Godmother, no magic left.

How bittersweet to get what you desire and still not be enough! A lesson I should have learned a long time ago, when I wore those fancy slippers to that ball, you'd say. But I didn't. You and I are proof of that. We both wanted this one thing—a piece of paradise, of heaven—and now we have had it… What's next?

You are in my thoughts. Please keep me in yours.

My dear sir,

I read your letter, and I'm sure my husband or his secretary will answer with the expected gilded, formal words. It'll all be done properly, as expected. I am not expected to write to you—these are matters of state, from a king to another. You didn't write to congratulate me for surviving the birth of a daughter—you wrote to the country to congratulate the sovereign for the birth of an heiress to the throne.

These are the words of the charwoman princess to the valiant tailor king. I couldn't choose her first name—my husband had the divine right to name his offspring as he pleased, and by law it is his offspring. But I chose her second name. She is Rose to me. She will always be Rose to me. And I hope that when you remember her—should you remember her—, that she will always be Rose to you, too.

We know for certain Schneider hadn't replied to the letters, since Cinderella passed away two weeks after the birth of her daughter. A month later, the Crown Prince was deposed in a coup d'état that led to the insurgence of a republic. One of the many rumours at the time linked Schneider's monetary help to the ascendance of the new order. This was reinforced when the Revolutionary Committee unveiled their new coat of arms: three roses tied with a strip of linen—the same sort of roses Schneider had offered to Cinderella many years before.

Anna Martino is an SF/F writer and editor based in São Paulo (Brazil), running **Dame Blanche**, a small press specialized in local speculative fiction. She has been published both in English and in Portuguese – her English work has been featured on BBC World Radio and, more recently, at *Translunar Travellers Lounge* (February 2020).

- THE BAD WIFE
- VASILISA THE WISE
- FANTASY

CURRANTS TO THE SEA

TARYN HAAS

Vasilisa had been married before. A wedding rushed by her father, hungry for a name to tie himself to. And an even hungrier husband, demanding first her body then her skills in quick succession.

Vasilisa was skilled in many things, but she still could not meet her husband's demands. She was skilled in falling asleep after he did what husbands do after a long day of work and drink; she was skilled in making friends of the goats so their cheese was the best in town; she was skilled in combining meat and potatoes and spices so the potatoes were ignored, saving them money.

But she was not skilled in anticipating her husband's needs. She could bear demands, but expectations without expression were impossible to fulfill.

It began with pancakes, of all things. Vasilisa prided herself on her pancakes. The first one cooked of course was always meant to test the pan. Each subsequent one came out perfect for its fluffiness and crisp outsides. How she wished someone would see her in both strength and softness.

But her husband was an enigma. He would come home hungry and find potatoes and sausage insufficient, then berate her for lack of pancakes with sweet syrup to drip from the edges of his plate.

So some days she tried to anticipate his need. One day, when they hadn't had pancakes for nearly a week, she made fifty pancakes crispy with butter and fluffy with eggs from their chickens. But when he arrived home, he scoffed, "I did not ask for pancakes! Why would you think I want these for dinner, today of all days?"

From that day forward, Vasilisa decided to do the opposite of whatever her husband asked. When he asked for his socks to be washed, she rubbed them in the mud. When he asked for her to come to bed, she cleaned the kitchen relentlessly until she bled into the scrubbing of pots and plates. When he said he was leaving for a week to trade in the nearby town and she was not to leave the house, she waited for the lock to turn in the front door before she stepped out the back.

The goats bleated happily at her as she passed their enclosure. The chickens stared at her with one eye, then the other, anticipation trembling in their red-encrusted throats. The grasses in the field waved to her, a husband's hand she never held.

She paused at the edge of the forest, the edge of the land he owned. The edge of the land she cultivated.

With her first step, the trees met her with grace. With the second, shadows accepted hers into their own. With the third, shadows and self no longer mattered.

Vasilisa was not sure how long she walked in the filtered sunlight, leaves sweeping their delight across her view with each few steps.

After hundreds of steps, she reached a currant bush with berries deep red in ripeness. And while she knew he was not here, she heard in her head,

Do not pick that bush.

The voice of her husband, invasive and controlling.

She paused, her hand cupping a bunch of berries that begged to fall into her palm.

There was no one else here in the woods with her, she assured herself.

Pulling the berries gently, they fell into her palm and followed the path of her hand to her mouth.

Their sweetness met her mouth with sour in turn. The sourness, she had to remind herself, was not her husband forcing himself into her mouth. It was just currants being currants.

Yet still, she heard his voice.

Do not enter the bush.

Determined to find unowned land, she forced her way through the thin harsh branches. They formed thick masses against her arms and legs, but she pressed forward.

Until she no longer had to press. With the words of her husband echoing in the leaves above her, an endless stream of *Do not go, do not go, do not—*

Her foot met emptiness, then her calf against air. As if tumbling off a cliff, her entire body rushing against air and darkness within the bush.

His voice echoing from the leaves behind her, their rustling fading to whispers.

Do not go, do not, how dare....

There was not an end, Vasilisa learned after an unknown time. She fell through anxiety, then desperation, then resolution. There was nothing to fear aside from falling, so she decided not to fear.

It felt like years of wind rushing against her ears, braiding her hair into intricate pieces, and a sense of calm that can only come in darkness. Yet even there, things lived. She tumbled into the view of pointed ears and an exaggerated nose. Its yellow imp eyes held hers despite whatever odd angles they reached in their fall together. Its moon-eyes seemed unblinking and curious in turn.

Vasilisa had heard of such creatures that lived in the darkness, and her heart thundered at the thought of offending it. She remained quiet, wondering if she had conjured the eyes just so she was not alone.

After uncountable moments, it spoke from an unseen mouth, "What brought you here?"

Its voice was soft, softer than the whispering bush that had become part of her past, softer than her hair brushed by wind, softer than the nothingness she fell through. Vasilisa was not sure if she had ever heard a voice made of down and moth's wings such as this.

Vasilisa took three days to respond to its question.

On the first, she thought the answer was fear. That she had run away from her husband because she was afraid of what he would become.

On the second, she thought the answer was pancakes. That she made such lovely pancakes, but never at the right time, and so she had wandered to see what she could do right.

On the third day, she answered without thinking.

"Myself."

And immediately thought how obvious an answer it was. Of course, no matter how or what, she had brought herself here.

But the imp considered, its moon eyes growing slightly smaller in its thought, then wider as it asked:

"What do you want?"

Vasilisa again took three days to respond.

On the first, she thought the answer was freedom. That she had run away from a cage and now she would create her own world.

On the second, she thought the answer was power. Power to control her own house, her own meals, her own existence.

On the third day, she answered without thinking.

"Acceptance."

The imp's eyes narrowed as their heads hurtled downward toward a ground they knew they would never meet.

"Do you trust me?"

The imp asked, and this time Vasilisa answered without hesitation.

"Yes."

Immediately she plunged into the sea, undercurrents rushing against her thighs and soft sand playing against her hair. She felt how upside down she was, that the sea could take her but hadn't. And that the imp had put her here for a purpose.

Vasilisa did not try to right herself. She was used to not breathing, as she had held her breath for hours and days within the currant bush. The waves pushed in and out and soon she felt their heart, a longing for the sand and sky but a marriage to the fish and coral.

The first day of holding her breath, Vasilisa watched sea turtles climb out of the froth to return hours later, eyes clear and limbs free as they pushed toward the depths.

The second day of holding her breath, Vasilisa watched the sun set and the moon rise, each light playing on soft waves at the surface in ways she could not imagine, for she had forgotten what breath was like.

The third day, Vasilisa turned herself down toward the depths of the ocean, for no longer was she afraid of what she could not breathe and she was fond of moving downwards.

There, she found wide green eyes framed with seaweed hair and a kingly crown, so unlike the yellowed eyes of the imp she knew.

"Vasilisa, you have turned to me," He drew her down to the darkness where his eyes glowed even brighter. "I do not know how you came to be here, but you are one of my daughters, a follower of the dark currents."

Vasilisa nodded, confident in herself but not in his eyes, too green and too focused.

"So you shall be. Follow, follow, daughter of mine."

For three weeks, the Sea King showed Vasilisa his domain, his coral palace and chariot of marlins. For each new view, Vasilisa made a point of showing her enjoyment. She was, truly, enjoying herself in the depths of the sea and the novelties it held. More, she knew that as a daughter of the king she would never be made his servant or wife. Here, the voice of her husband could not quite reach her, making it only as far as words played in the oldest of sea grasses.

Come...belong...me....

On the third day of the third week, the Sea King brought Vasilisa to the surface of the shore with his eleven other daughters in identical dresses. They hung suspended in a clear pool of water before a young woman with an eagle at her side. The eagle opened his mouth and cried, "This princess has fed me, sold her fortune to keep me alive and led me here. You want one worthy of your daughters, and here I present such."

Vasilisa felt the shudder of the Sea King's laugh in the water, unseen on the shore. It was true, the princess had a thin frame, emaciated with eyes too large for her face, and cheekbones that went beyond pronounced. Yet still Vasilisa felt her heart trill slightly, a note of a flute somewhere far beneath her that betrayed the mirror of those hungry eyes. A hunger that would be sated with soft touches and sweet foods.

"Daughters," the Sea King cried, "She shall have the pick of you, should she pass my trials. The first task: build me a great crystal bridge!"

Her heart dropping, Vasilisa descended with her new sisters, all of them gossiping of her ribcage and the idiocy of the eagle to trust someone so weak.

"She fed that which was not her's." Vasilisa protested, but her words were swallowed by a school of mackerel, twisting and turning in silver variations.

As they dined that first night, the Sea King raised a glass. "To our new crystal bridge, should she build such a thing!"

Vasilisa raised her glass but did not sip when it reached her mouth. She knew nothing of bridges, but she knew of crystal as it had lined the quarries of her town. While her sisters and father drank glass after glass of bubbling champagne, Vasilisa imagined supports of clear blue, arches of crystal meeting as hands holding for eternity.

Rising up to the sandy coast, she found the princess sleeping on a cloak of midnight blue. Without waking her, she whispered in her ear the construction she imagined and how she might accomplish it by morning. No sooner had she slipped into the sea than the princess awoke, enlivened by how she would meet the Sea King's challenge.

On her way back down, she heard a voice in the anemones, swaying to

Where is my wife, where is mine, where has my....

Vasilisa swam away, pushing the voice from her mind.

When the sun was fully in the sky, Vasilisa and her eleven sisters rose with their Sea King to the surface, smug expressions on all but one. Crowns broke the surface to see an expanse of crystal, wide enough for two carriages, leaping across their sea.

The Sea King approached the princess, a blank expression pressed on his face. "You have completed this, and proved you are perhaps worthy of one of my daughters. But I am not yet convinced. By tomorrow morning, you must turn the barren landscape upon which you sleep into a garden of such renown that people from across the world shall wish for the fruit and flowers you have sown."

The princess said nothing, simply nodded with her wide eyes. The Sea King and his daughters slipped into the sea to drink and cheer that such a garden had never been made and would never be. But Vasilisa again held a drink to her lips without swallowing and thought of the girl with hollow cheeks. How apples and peaches and plums might fill them out. So while the others drank their fill, she rose to the surface where she found the princess asleep. Rather than whisper in her ear, she pulled herself onto the sand. She whispered into each seed buried in the loamy soil of their destiny to grow strong and huge, to form fruit that might capture the rays reflected from the moon. Throughout the night, she repeated the story of each seed to itself, of what it might and should be.

With the lightest of blues reaching into the sky, she slipped herself back into the darkness of the waves.

On the way back down to her sisters, Vasilisa heard the kelp lifting a tiny voice

No matter, no matter, hands are bodies are mine are bodies....

At full dawn, the Sea King and his daughters rose to see if the princess had managed his task. The smirk on the king's face was enough to know what he expected. To grow a garden before light had struck was impossible.

Yet, as they all rose, they were awed with broad branches and thick fruit clinging to the tips of the trees. Vasilisa hid her smile, impressed that her words had held such power with mere seeds.

The princess presented herself to the Sea King, bowing as she said "Your task is done. What more do you wish of me?"

The Sea King paused, then said cautiously, "You have earned one of my daughters. But as you see, I have many daughters. You may only have one of them should you choose the same daughter thrice; they are face for face, hair for hair, dress for dress. Should you fail, you will have none."

Vasilisa again felt her heart trill at the thought she might fail, that her wide white eyes would never meet the princess' again, that she would never again whisper in her ear great plans or work for their delight in the morning.

That night as her father and eleven sisters drank their fill of bubbles, Vasilisa slipped away to the twilights of currents. She reached the princess before she could fall asleep on the sand, telling her quickly "handkerchief, dress, fly" before she was pulled back to the songs and dances of her sisters.

On the way down she heard the sound of red algae, sad and high as it cried softly

Why me...why me...why me....

In the morning, the twelve daughters were presented to the princess thrice. For the first, Vasilisa flicked the handkerchief in her hand, and the princess pointed to her. For the second, Vasilisa adjusted her dress to cover both of her shoulders rather than dip to upper arms as her sisters positioned their's. Again, the princess pointed to Vasilisa.

For the third, Vasilisa had placed a small piece of crab from last night's dinner into her hair. A fly swirled around her head, drawn to the rancid smell that her sisters barely managed to ignore, their glances at her disgusted and hateful. Again the princess pointed to Vasilisa.

The Sea King had no desire to let go of Vasilisa, so hard won through both the imp and a portal that he thought would never result in anything worthwhile. Yet here she was, and so quick to leave. Perhaps that was the fate for one so eager to tumble with white eyes. And the Sea King had made a deal with the princess and the eagle, one he knew he could not rescind.

Vasilisa returned to the sand from the sea, pulling breath shallowly from the air around her. This would take work, she knew, but breathing could be learned.

As she moved from one world to another, she heard the tiny clams beneath her bubbling

Free I am free I am free...he is...thank you knife....

She took the princess's hand and together they became Queens in the land of their garden, a crystal bridge bringing trade and life. Their cheeks grew fat with plums, their ribs lined with peaches and apples. They spread currant seeds across their forests, hoping that no one would feel so hopeless here as to enter the endless fall. But never would Vasilisa live in a land without doors to freedom. She trusted the imp would be there to take worthy individuals to currents that held each person in calm embraces so they could see the yellow of sky against foam, the stars echoed in deep water, and a reflection of acceptance given unconditionally.

Taryn Haas received their undergrad in Philosophy from the University of Pittsburgh in 2015. They have since escaped to Vermont, which is basically a way better version of PA. They live with their husband; 3 dogs Locke, Kafka, and Pippin; cat, Duncan Idaho; and crested gecko, Azula. They are a student at Vermont College of Fine Arts in the Creative Writing for Children and Young Adults program. While they spend most of their time on work and school, they also enjoy snowboarding, hiking, dog agility, and baking scones. They identify as nonbinary and queer. Their website is tarynhaas.net.

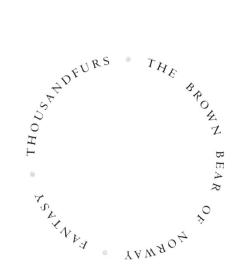

THOUSANDFURS • THE BROWN BEAR OF NORWAY • FANTASY

CLOAK OF BEARSKIN

ANNA MADDEN

The well was lined with cracks, smelling of mildew and sun-drenched stone. Vera watched a blackbird land on the rim. Its eyes were human-like.

Vera drew up the well bucket. Nearby, chickens hunted insects in the kitchen yard, and smoke curled from the earth stove. Its coals burned ember-red.

Rosemary called over. She carried two speckled brown hens, asleep forevermore. "We've a guest tonight, so I'd best do the seasoning."

Horseshoes struck cobblestone. A horseman approached, his cloak dust-covered. He had a tall nose, dark eyes, and limbs well-suited to riding attire.

Rosemary tugged Vera's sleeve. "Don't stare."

Dazed, Vera plucked the hens and wondered what brought the horseman to Ursine, a kingdom once well-regarded but now ensorcelled. Who was he, then? Scents of cut onion and fresh bread signaled opportunity.

Vera cleared her throat. "I'll deliver the food."

"The state you're in," Rosemary said, "you'd drop the platter. Go to bed."

⋯●⋯

Vera woke to sounds in the night. A growl rattled the door. The bar had been placed as usual, but the timber was old, half-rotted.

The servants whimpered. "My lady," the oldest said, "you don't think—"

"Don't fret," she said, trying to sound calm, though in truth she wished Rosemary were there, but the cook slept in the stables. "Maybe a coyote got into the coop. I'll look."

Through the window, moonlight highlighted the yard. The well's shadow was larger than usual. It moved, walking on four paws.

Vera gasped. "There's a bear chained up outside."

⋯●⋯

At dawn, the chains were empty. As Vera walked toward the stables, she saw large claw prints in the dirt.

The stables smelled of hay and oats and manure. The rider's steed was inside the largest stall. A proud gelding with a black mane. Vera offered a carrot. The horse eyed her, then accepted the treat as if ashamed of himself. A feeling Vera knew too well.

"Carrots are Flint's favorite."

Vera spun. The rider watched her. He looked weary. A cloak of bearskin hung off his back. It was elaborate, made of many furs. Staring, Vera pictured a bear with knife-like claws. She shuddered.

The man held his hands out. "I frightened Flint, too. It's like he's forgotten me." He looked closer at Vera. "Who are you?"

"I'm a poor girl," Vera said, "who has no mother or father." Pale, sun-kissed hair hid her face.

The rider leaned closer. Flint snorted and pawed the dirt floor. Vera suspected the horse smelled a bear. She did. Her heart pounded. She fled, passing Weston, the stablemaster, and forced herself to walk slower.

"Pull his shoes and turn him out to green pasture," the rider said to Weston. "I'll be staying."

Under the sun, Vera came face-to-face with Starling. By her magic, the witch had gained control of Ursine and orphaned Vera, keeping her hale but locked into servitude. Any day, Starling might turn Vera into a blackbird too.

Starling frowned at Vera. "What use are you, avoiding your chores?" Her voice spilled like honey, sticky, easy to get trapped within. The air grew heavy with magic: a scent of burnt feathers and lilacs.

Vera dipped her shoulders. "I'm worthless. Good for nothing."

Starling nodded, a smile on her lips. The scent of magic weakened.

⋅•⋅

At midday, Vera helped hang white linen to bleach in sunlight. She asked about the visitor.

"Prince Bruin?" Tansy said, a maid close in height to Vera but with rounder cheeks. "His land suffers from blight. He's searching for a cure, and Starling fancies him. Who wouldn't? He's tall and rich."

"She likes him?" Vera asked, hiding her disappointment with a bedsheet.

"She must," Tansy said. "She gifted him a fine fur cloak."

A blackbird cawed. Looking at it, Tansy turned bone-white. Vera took Tansy's hand. The blackbird could easily have been Fern—Tansy's betrothed.

Tansy squeezed back. "I overheard their bargain: if he dons the cloak each night for a whole season, the witch promised to reveal the name of his bride: a girl as warm as the sun. Their marriage will cure the blight. If he breaks the pact, though, he must marry Starling instead."

Vera sighed. She was tired of living this way, in fear, seeing all she loved turned to wing and beak and claw. "I must fix this, somehow."

・●・

As the evening meal cooked, Vera asked Rosemary for clusters of dried lavender. "To help us sleep."

Rosemary nodded, dark crescents shadowing her eyes. "I'll make chamomile tea. See everyone gets some."

That night, between the lavender and the chamomile, snores echoed across the kitchen. Vera's heartbeat thundered. A chain rattled. Next, the bear growled. Vera tiptoed through the sleeping servants to the window.

Outside, the prince ambled on four feet. She recognized his gait, so noble, full of grace despite his enchanted form. He paced. Metal rung when he tugged against his short chain. He suffered until daybreak, then fell to his side, human again with the fur cloak on his back.

The servants slept soundly. Vera lowered the bar on the kitchen door, quietly, then slipped outside. Wings of blackbirds stirred, and she froze, for Weston stood in the yard, but his back was turned. He unchained Prince Bruin and helped him to his feet.

Vera took a shortcut to the keep. She entered a guest bedroom. There was a large fireplace with an iron grate and a four-post bed. She hid under its massive frame.

The door opened. Vera put a hand over her mouth to quiet her breaths. The bear cloak fell in a heap over thick rugs. Vera could see the prince's bare feet. He shut the door, which didn't quite latch.

"Come out," he said. His words held no magic, but they were stern, full of authority.

Vera obeyed.

"I recognize you," Prince Bruin said. His clothes were torn and dirty. "You were kind to Flint."

Vera met his eyeline. "I came for the cloak of bearskin."

He considered her. "What for?"

"To burn it," she said without hesitation.

"If you do that, Starling wins," Prince Bruin said. "I can't keep my promise without it."

"Starling tricked you," Vera said, "same as my father. That cloak will make you forget who you are or why you came here."

The prince touched Vera's hair. "It's golden like Queen Aurum's. You're her daughter, the king's heir?"

"I'm—" Vera stared into his dark eyes, so piercing, and faltered, realizing she had almost given the same answer as before.

"I think it's you who've forgotten who you are," Prince Bruin said. "I've heard of you, Vera."

Vera stiffened when he spoke her name.

"You were sick five years ago," he said, "and the witch cured you, though it cost your parents their lives. I've been instructed in the basics of magic. A healing spell is unique—Starling is bound by her magic, just as I am bound to wear the cloak. She can't hurt you."

"Even if that's true," Vera said, "she can hurt others. She turns the servants into blackbirds, and now you, into a bear."

Prince Bruin took her hand in his. "A price I'll willingly pay. I should have realized when I saw your hair and the sunlight you carry in your heart. You're who I've been searching for."

Vera flushed, and Prince Bruin kissed her. His lips tasted soft and true. In that moment, Vera remembered herself and the power of a king's blood.

A faint noise at the door broke them apart. It creaked open. Starling was there. Her expression was ice and fire. She tried to slap Vera, but she couldn't, and pain lined her face. If Vera had challenged her before, would the others have suffered? She swallowed. The prince had reminded her of her own worth, her own voice.

With care, Vera spoke. "Release the servants, then take the cloak of bearskin and leave us. You'll wear it every day for five years."

The witch paled. She picked up the fur cloak and left.

The prince waited. This time, Vera kissed him. An answer more powerful than words. She pulled away.

"How did you know I was under the bed?" Vera asked.

Prince Bruin laughed. "You smell of lavender and chamomile. Quite strongly. My nose is sensitive since becoming a bear."

Vera heard crying. Sharing a look with Prince Bruin, she hurried outside. Tansy's face was tear-streaked, her arms around Fern who was human again. Rosemary and Weston danced, and the other servants formed a circle, their voices lifted in song. The cobblestones were covered in black feathers.

With light steps, Vera went to the well and looked into its heart. She made a wish for a wedding dress as silvery as the moon, as bright as the stars. A dress for a king's daughter.

Anna Madden lives in Fort Worth, Texas. Her fiction has appeared in *DreamForge Magazine*, where she also volunteers as a First Line Reader. Upcoming short stories will be published with *Dark Matter Magazine* and *Hybrid Fiction*. She has a Bachelor of Arts: English degree with a creative writing emphasis from the University of Missouri - Kansas City. To learn more, visit her website at annamadden.com.

DONKEYSKIN • THE LITTLE MERMAID • SOLARPUNK

SUNSHINE NOIR FOR SYNTHETIC LOVERS

LIN DARROW

When Jin slipped out of bed in the morning, his coat slipped onto him. He had only to settle his feet over the cracks in the floorboards, where the agriyet vines leeched through, and wait for them to climb up the backs of his calves, thread over his spine, and knit together into a long, frayed coat. A rich man would have kept his threads in neat little pots and pods built into the walls, or even threaded the living vine through the wallpaper. But Jin lived on the wrong side of Ersepheo's Wilting Way, where nobody could afford that kind of luxury.

On days when the vines were undernourished or too weak to make the climb, he would crawl out to the fire escape and steal the rest of a shirt from the wild agriyet blanketing his apartment building. Then, as it threaded itself around his narrow frame, he would watch the sunlight lance its rays across Ersepheo's jagged glass horizon.

The agriyet vine leeched over everything in the Wilting Way. It soaked the entire district in the colours of a sick heart, from cylindrical skyscrapers to streetcar ceilings to neon signage for sun specs and 'dark' bars. If he looked very hard, he could see the soft purple misteria vines of the wealthy Garland district, the bright lime ivy drenching the hipper Sprigtown, the deep red briars designating the Thorne district. That was probably the nicest thing anyone had ever said about the Wilting Way: it had a real swell view of other, greener, more sun-kissed districts.

That morning, as Jin felt his way through the sun-starved rot to find a patch of agriyet that wasn't dying, he cast his usual look out at the Wilting Way. Across the street from his apartment was a billboard, which had read **'MASON PYRE FOR MAYOR! 56 PERCENT ORGANIC, 100 PERCENT DEVOTED TO ERSEPHEO!'** the night before.

The billboard had changed. It now read:

'LOSE YOUR HEART TO OCTAVIA BARD, THE SUNBURST CLUB'S SWEET SYNTHETIC SYNCOPATOR!'

"Gender-wise, she's 68 percent synth, right?" came a low, lilting voice from the balcony opposite the fire escape. Jin turned, midway through lighting a cigarette, to see his neighbour, Elsie, leaning over the rail. She'd evidently splurged on a bit of ironflower vine recently, and had woven it into a soft morning robe around her plump figure. At 58 percent, she was just organic enough to be able to host more delicate, fashionable fauna, but her eyes still had the same dull blue synthetic glow as Jin's own.

"What of it?" Jin asked, a little prickly as the poisonous twinge of the agriyet settled into his marrow, taking root for the day. In exchange for the uncomfortable snap of poison in what little blood he could boast having, the agriyet leaves would leech up sun and power the synthetic limbs of his skeleton.

"A 68-S is downright workable with a face like that," Elsie said, lifting a cigarette to her lips. "You never told me how pretty he is!"

"Wouldn't know," Jin said, glancing darkly up at the billboard, where Octavia Bard's red lipstick and evening gown made from emerald root sparkled obnoxiously in the sun. "I'm 88-S, remember?"

"Forget that," Elsie laughed. "You got eyes, don't you?"

Jin wilted over the railing and tossed his cigarette into his downstairs neighbour's blue clover patch. It was easy for Elsie to flirt around the idea, he thought bitterly, as he headed down to the street to catch the streetcar covered in sun-sucking rye moss. At 58-O, she could be openly attracted to either gender: those over 50 percent organic (who used 'she'), or those over 50 percent synthetic (who used 'he'). She was just close enough to the threshold that a certain bohemian androgyny let her get away with it. But Jin, with his stalwart 88-S/12-O balance, was ranked decisively synthetic, which made any hypothetical interest in another S-designation socially taboo.

It was a problem, people like Mason Pyre loved to say—usually while standing at a podium and clutching her 56-S trophy husband by the waist—when both parents' genders leaned too far in one direction. Not enough genetic diversity. Too synthetic, and you relied too much on the solar power provided by Ersepheo's symbiotic fauna. Too organic, and you were too vulnerable to contagion, vine-poisoning, and disease. 'Give the child a chance at the elusive 50-50 ideal!' Pyre would cry into every campaign microphone that would wilt her way. And if there were to be no children, no new bodies to ensure the symbiotic Ersepheo fauna could continue to flourish and generate power, then why partner at all? What good did it do society?

So, on record, Jin did not think about Octavia Bard.

Which was difficult, the ardent not-thinking, when he went to work every day at the Sunburst Club.

The Sunburst was a dark club in Sprigtown, which meant that its windows were painted black to keep out Ersepheo's 42-hour sunlight. Every night, Octavia sang three songs to rapturous applause: *When the Sun Gets In Your Eyes*, *Red Rose Blues*, and *My Sweet Synthetic Beau*. It was Jin's job to help Octavia into the kaleidoscope of flora-woven evening gowns donated to the club by lovestruck organic-leaning patrons, and a few particularly daring synthetics close to the threshold.

Octavia liked to host gigantic bird-of-paradise flowered gowns, the living stalks kept in vases at his vanity. On his plump hourglass frame it was complicated and ornate, which meant he needed help pulling the hosted fibres from his skin when he was finished, and Jin—ostensibly security—had the biggest hands in the place.

"Arrghhh, I feel like a walking billboard for something explosive," he would gripe, which would make Jin laugh, because Octavia had a gift for comparison and came prepared with a new one every day.

That day, it was, "I look like target practice for somebody who viscerally hates birds and/or the abstract concept of paradise."

Jin bit his lip and tried hard not to laugh, but his shoulders shook from the effort, and his fingers grew clumsy with the fibrous knots of the flower stems.

"Careful!" Octavia laughed, reaching back to press his hand over Jin's, where he had pulled too tightly at Octavia's waistline. "Sorry, I shouldn't be funny. Though you're equally at fault for your good sense of humour, I suppose."

He smiled back at him, long eyelashes and red lipstick over one soft synthetic shoulder.

"I'll try to shake it somehow," Jin said softly, because while he knew how to laugh, he was less skilled at banter.

It wasn't that Octavia was beautiful. That was a given, considering his 68-S designation: decidedly synthetic, but still genetically diverse enough to be attractive partner to somebody leaning the opposite way. Maybe not for would-be mayoral hopefuls like Mason Pyre, but enough to make some minor official with an organic leaning in the 60s happy enough. It wasn't even that he had a voice as soft and sparkling as a dragonfly's wings, or a dramatic eye for organic fashion that had designated him Ersepheo's floral-wear icon.

What made Octavia hard to stop thinking on was this. All of Octavia's lovers, from the minor politicians to the garden-planners of the greener districts, did not know how funny he was, or how he could make the dullest things sound enchanting with a well-dolloped word. Because Octavia Bard on stage—and he was always 'on stage', even when dining out at garden parties or attending the flower operas in the Garland district—was an entirely different entity than Octavia Bard backstage.

That Jin did know the difference was his most miserably cherished secret.

"I guess my time's up," Octavia said one day, after Jin had returned the bird-of-paradise vines to their vases. He sat in a fluffy robe of rubiyet moss, smoking out the window. "I can't keep ducking roots forever, you know. Not in this sun-bleached town."

"You're only 38," Jin replied.

"You're desperately sweet," Octavia replied, exhaling vaporous smoke. "Tragically, I'm just organic enough to wrinkle, and while I think the dark circles give me a certain smoky air of experience—well, experience is much harder to market. All the fat cat 50s need to feel like they're rescuing you, you know. Blessing you with their good genetics, and loftily overlooking yours."

This was too much to bear, and Jin worried Octavia could see it in his clenched jaw. He scratched at his beard, the roots of which were leeched with reddish dye from the agriyet.

"So who's the lucky sap?" he asked, after he'd gained control of himself.

There were a few options: Jared Pyre, daughter of Mason Pyre, up-and-coming councillor, a 62-O. Maybe Nia Carroway, 65-O, a frequent patron who owned a rather profitable sun-spectacle business. Or worse yet, it could be Carlton Mayhew, an insufferable 51-O soprano from the flower opera, who had a career simply by virtue of her near-perfect balance.

Octavia considered the question.

"Someone reliable, and gentle, if a little shy," he said at length. "Know anyone?"

Jin ducked his head.

Octavia sighed, and reached to hold Jin's big hands in his smaller ones. For a moment, he simply held them. Then he reached to pluck a clover from the pot on the windowsill, and knotted it around Jin's finger.

"Decide for me, will you, darling?" he said. "I haven't the heart to do it myself. Anyone who wears this ring, I'll accept. So choose well."

Jin looked to his hand. It may as well have been a curse.

• • •

It was during the single hour of night that Ersepheo experienced after 42 hours of sun that Jin finally worked up the courage to see the Tailor.

The Tailor, it was said, was a tragic marvel of nature: 100 percent organic. She kept a shop by the lilac bridge down on Cloverside, one with no sign on the window. The door only opened if you knew the password: *I seek three dresses the colour of the sky, the moon, and the sun.*

"The cinderskin flower takes deep root," said the Tailor, her face surrounded by endless waterfalls of red vines. "It will thread itself upon your frame like a fine cloak, and it will change your leaning. You will slowly become more and more organic as it embraces you, threads itself within you."

A hand emerged from the falling vines, holding an amethyst-coloured flower between two fingers. Jin reached for it, but the Tailor drew it back.

"But know this," she warned him. "It is a jealous bloom. It will chase all other fauna from your body. No agriyet will take root in you, and you will play host to no other sun-drinking flower. This will decimate your synthetic body. The joints in your jaw, the vocal chip that allows you to speak, the power cells in your legs. The weight of this disguise is great."

"If it changes my leaning legitimately, how can you call it a disguise?" Jin asked.

"Because you will not recognize yourself," the Tailor replied. "You will live forever in this second skin. If ever you remove the cloak it makes for you, you will starve from lack of sunlight, do you understand? Your body will be made fit to host only the cinderskin."

"I understand," Jin said, as he took the flower, set it on his tongue, and let it weave its roots deep into him.

It was a gradual change, and took almost an entire sun-cycle. He lay in bed and writhed with the pain of it, as the cinderskin threaded itself through the organic cells of his skin, rooting itself along his synthetic skeleton like endless rows of leafy teeth. The leaves drank thirstily from the meagre sun in his apartment, powering him with just enough energy to toss and turn from the agony.

At last, one day Jin looked in the mirror and thought of himself as herself. Without needing to check, she knew she had passed the 50 percent organic threshold. The cinderskin had swept her frame in complex waves of purple vine. It had flowered in her beard, swept up her neck in a tall collar, and fallen down her back again in a layered gown and cloak. It framed her face in heart-shaped leaves, and dyed her eyes a deep, poisoned colour. When she swallowed, the feeling was wetter than before, and she felt the cinderskin bulb brush the roof of her mouth.

"There is one more caveat," the Tailor had said, just before Jin took the flower. "Your lips never touch another's, for the originating bulb will sit forever on your tongue. It will extend to a second host if the proximity is allowed."

Jin looked down at her hand. The clover ring was still there, buried under a ruffle of leaves.

• • •

The flower opera in Garland was a grand glass building covered in candy-coloured misteria. Jin hurried up the endless steps, her long coat and skirts layered with purple-red cinderskin leaves in various bleeding tones. She came upon Octavia on the grand staircase, which was drizzled in rainbow-toned vines and blossoms like the cascading bounty of twin treasure boxes.

Octavia wore a gown woven entirely from palicourea elata, kiss-shaped flowers that were delicate and tricky to host—a near-obnoxious display of his skill at weaving.

"Hello," Jin tried to say, only the bulb tightened on her tongue, and she realized that the roots had knotted around her voice box.

Octavia, glancing her over, smiled.

"I've never seen that colour in an Ersepheo vine," he said admiringly.

With no words, Jin floundered. Then she raised her hand, indicating the ring.

Octavia's eyes widened. Then his expression shuttered.

"Well," he said. "I suppose I did promise, even though I consider Jin Ledo to be a rogue of the worst sort, leaving me for *months* with no word… and no dresser! Shall we sit together, then?"

They took a box together that looked out over the garden that comprised the stage, and suffered through Carlton Mayhew's ear-blasting aria. Octavia coolly smoked a vapor cigarette in a long holder, while Jin, sitting nervously at his side, spent more time looking at the pink hydrangea gown Mayhew was hosting.

As though reading her mind, Octavia said, dryly, "It's a good thing my eardrums aren't litigious. I have more notes on that dress than she's hit in an hour."

Jin's shoulders shook with silent laughter. Octavia turned to her.

"It is you," he said warmly. "Jin."

Jin froze.

Octavia grinned, and reached to touch the blossoms in Jin's beard. "You always were the only one who found me funny."

Heart hammering with new blood, Jin leapt to her feet in a flurry of shivering vines.

"You knew?" she mouthed.

"It took me a minute. But the ash clover, once knotted, cannot be removed," Octavia said, setting the cigarette holder aside. "I was trying to tell you—oh, this is embarrassing—that I wouldn't marry *anyone else*. I should have known you'd take me literally. You're so single-minded and stalwart that way."

Jin flushed through the curling vine.

"What have you done to yourself?" Octavia asked. "How are you hosting this much vine?"

Sheepishly, Jin opened her mouth. Octavia stood, framed her face with his hands, and peered inside.

"You took the cinderskin flower," he lamented. His expression twisted. "You fool! You left me for *months* for this?! It's the world that needs to change, not you."

"I don't care about my gender, I never have, but everyone else *does*," Jin tried to say, but this was too much for Octavia to piece out. So she mouthed a different phrase instead, which only took three simple syllables.

Octavia's expression softened. He stroked his fingers through Jin's beard.

"If I'm not careful, it will take root in me, too, right?"

Jin nodded miserably. It sat silently between them then. If Octavia also hosted the cinderskin, then eventually they would both lean too far organic, and arrive back at the same problem that had prompted Jin to seek out the Tailor in the first place.

"I don't know how you expect me to suffer through a lifetime without kissing you," Octavia said, interrupting Jin's grim line of thought.

Jin began to shake her head and mouthed, "It's selfish. It's *wrong.*"

"According to whom?" Octavia asked.

"Everyone," Jin wanted to say. "The world."

It must have read on her face anyway, because Octavia smiled softly.

"The old world must hurt to bring the new into being," he said.

Jin looked away, ashamed of Octavia's bravery.

At last she gestured to her throat and mouthed, "You'll lose your voice."

"And gain an opulent cinderskin dress!" Octavia countered flippantly. He touched the clover ring on Jin's hand. "Though I'd have accepted a simpler vine from you, I hope you know."

Jin clasped him in her arms and held him tighter than she'd ever held anything. She felt Octavia's smaller fingers trail up her back. Then, before she could think of any further objections, Octavia drew her back, and pressed his lips to hers. They kissed in the quiet dark of intermission, to the distant sound of audience applause.

When they drew back, Octavia's lips were tinged a poisonous hue. Jin's heart hammered out a melody that felt a little like the sting of agriyet in the blood.

"If it's between that and a Mason Pyre-approved wedding, I can't say it's much of a choice at all, quite frankly," Octavia said, breaking the romance of the moment. "Wasn't planning on inviting her anyway."

Disarmed, Jin let out a silent laugh that rang with all the bubbling joy of organic things, through her softening lungs, her barrelling blood, and all the riotous fireworks of a working nervous system.

Dizzy from the feeling, she took Octavia's face in her hands, and drew him back for a second sin.

Lin Darrow holds a PhD in Victorian literature She wrote Slipshine Studio's award-winning sci-fi comic *Captain Imani and the Cosmic Chase*, as well as *Mysteries of the Spectral Hour*. She is the author of the webcomic *Shaderunners* (published by Hiveworks Comics), and has written prose stories and comics for anthologies such as *Valor: Cups and Valor: Wands, QueerSciFi, Malaise, Come Together!, Heartwood: Sylvan Tales of Non-Binary Fantasy, Tabula Idem*, and *Moonlight*. Her first novella, *Pyre at the Eyreholme Trust*, combined noir and fantasy, and was published by Less Than Three Press in 2018. Lin is based in Canada.

THE CANDLEWOOD TRAIL

DENNIS MOMBAUER

Lashkina was going home. She took a deep breath of the candleworld's resinous atmosphere and allowed a smile to pass over her lips. She was going home.

The serfs hauled the last crates aboard the space carriage and tightened the ropes. They had cut a good yield of candlewood and filled the carriage's storerooms to the brim, exceeding all expectations.

"Close the shutters." Lashkina supervised the preparations and looked out for any stragglers. "Secure the cargo and our equipment. We are leaving."

The whole carriage trembled as the chimneys fired up, and Lashkina held on to the lintel as she closed the last door. Smoke billowed through the paneled passageways as she made her way into the communal hall, where the serfs pulled scarves over their faces. The carriage rumbled skyward, and the candlewood world shrunk behind windows of stained glass.

Lashkina felt weightless as her stomach convulsed underneath her skin. Every contraction brought her closer to finishing this journey, her last delivery for her step-company. She would pay off her debts and be free.

"Congratulations, everyone." Her smile propagated itself through the assembled serfs, barely visible beneath their scarves. "Our harvest was plentiful, and we are well on time. This trip was worth it, for all of us. Thank you for your hard work."

The priest Kularev lit incense sticks and mumbled his prayers. The carriage stabilized, and the serfs dispersed into its corridors and chambers.

Outside the windows, the stars went out.

• •

Lashkina's throat closed and took away her breath. She blinked, but it remained dark outside the windows, utterly dark. The stars couldn't just vanish. It was an illusion, the shadow of a planet blocking out the great taiga of space, some rare astronomical event.

The carriage still careened forward with roaring chimneys, but it traveled blindly. The void rustled around them, pattered against the roof with slender branches. Someone inside the carriage howled, another wailed.

The darkness suffocated Lashkina. Every time she exhaled, she leaked more air she couldn't replace, as if something pulled it out with iron pliers.

"Please, everyone, stay calm. This will pass, it has to. Light the lanterns and don't despair."

Spots of brightness flared up along the soot-stained hallways. The windows remained black voids, but the carriage's lanterns provided a small measure of light.

Lashkina rushed toward her navigators and gesticulated to the priest Kularev to join them. "On our way to the candleworld, we passed an illuminated shrine. A statue of Saint Agathova, right? Can you get us there?"

The navigators nodded. Kularev opened his prayer book and read gibberish from its pages: "I was traveling post during a thaw, twelve leagues from the posting station. My cart comprised two hundred souls half-seated at full speed." He snapped it shut. "Yes. We will navigate from memory."

"Thank you." Lashkina let them get to work while she surveyed the hall. It was uncomfortable to sit here surrounded by vanished stars, the carriage visible from a great distance to anyone outside. Lashkina paced back and forth, trying to discern something outside the windows. "Chart the route. Get us home."

● ● ●

The carriage charged, and everyone inside the communal hall cheered. The taiga brushed over the walls, and the lanterns swayed as a sign of their passage.

Lashkina allowed herself some hope. If they reached the shrine, they were halfway home. The stars had gone out here, but they couldn't have gone out everywhere.

Lashkina walked through the carriage and spoke to the serfs. Most of them crouched on the benches or lined the walls, looking at her with fear and expectation. The company had placed them under her care, and she was not going to let them down.

"Everything is fine. I don't know what has happened, but I will get us back home."

"There was a presence on the world of candlewood." One serf addressed her in a low sing-song, and others joined in: "We have seen owl-birds perched on the branches. The swaths we cut grew over as we looked away. They twisted into directions we hadn't come from."

"So why is this the first I hear about it?"

"It didn't add up to anything, no? We got in and did our work, we came out with the harvest. What are some watching birds? What is some grass sprouting on the path?"

They had a point. With a yield like this, the company wouldn't ask questions: its representatives would smile, lick their lips, and release Lashkina from the contract. For the first time since her birth company perished, she would be free.

"A shivering expression was foaled in the slopes that took on the color of home." Kularev appeared next to Lashkina, his face obscured by his surging cassock. "The snow-clad ridge of this particular cart was a coarse ascent of insignificant persons in harness." He closed his prayer book. "We have a problem. There is a crossroad, and I don't know the right path."

"What are the options?" Lashkina shivered. If they chose the wrong path, they would get lost in the wilderness of space and never find their way back: if they didn't choose, they would wait here till their food and water ran out, a horsefly enclosed in a vein of coal.

• • •

"The dignities of a rustling silk stream. Sleepy eyes crowned by virtue of their inaccessible mountains." Kularev recited from his book like he was holding a mass. "They both look identical to me. One might be easier for the carriage to maneuver."

Lashkina remembered a rough ride when they had come, a shaky passage through turbulence. "Kularev, you don't remember? What about you navigators?"

The responsibility lay in her hands alone, and Lashkina fidgeted around with it. It was slippery and alive, digging into her palms with tiny barbs, tearing off strips of skin whenever she moved. "We take the harder road."

Kularev's beard bristled and belied the murkiness of his eyes. Lashkina was sure that part of him hoped for her to fail, that he waited for her to demonstrate she wasn't able to lead.

The priest knew his craft, but Lashkina needed to keep him on a short leash. She clenched her jaws: what was she thinking? That was company language, company strategy, company corruption. She needed to get out before it was too late.

"We take the harder road, and it will bring us to the shrine."

The chimneys stuttered and belched smoke as the carriage turned, trampling the undergrowth of star winds and chiming nebulae. "Down below roll remarkable faces."

"Light!" The serfs crowded around the windows, and the stained glass tattooed their faces with figures and symbols. "There is light!"

The void outside filled with brightness like a cloudy beer, a mélange of yellow liquid and floating sediment. The taiga still missed stars, but it regained its trees and bushes as the carriage completed the first leg of its journey.

• • •

A dome surrounded by columns and gilded wings appeared from the gloom. A frame of cypress logs housed the icon, a rotating figure of coal and encaustic wax. Saint Agathova, the patron of wanderers and woodcutters. Everlasting flames illuminated its garments and cast light into the twisting mists of space.

They had made it. Lashkina suppressed a smile, but it transformed the inside of her lips. They had escaped the star-less darkness, and now they only needed to press on.

The serfs racked up the carriage next to the shrine, and several ropes held it in place. Kularev copied passages from the shrine's glass-encased pages into his prayer book. "At an immense height, the brigades sang zealously, and the top of their voices seemed weary in the provinces," He nodded. "Let us congregate. Thank St. Agathova for its guidance. We will get home yet."

"Let's not waste time. Everyone who wants to pray can do so, but we leave right after."

A breath seemed to blow over the shrine, a spindly hand with too many fingers. The flames flickered.

"No. What is this?" Lashkina muttered to herself while the serfs froze halfway to their prayer positions. "It cannot be."

Another breath howled over the shrine, and this time, it was stronger. At one stroke, the everlasting flames extinguished, and the gilded angels fell into darkness. Like the stars, the Saint disappeared, and only the frayed ends of the ropes hung from the carriage.

This was madness. Lashkina held on to the polished wood of the wall. The serfs scrambled back into the carriage in panic, their pupils suddenly dilated and glistening in the void. Lashkina tried to impose order: "Everyone, to your stations! Fire up the chimneys."

People stumbled at the sudden acceleration and grabbed for the nearest object or person. No one could see anything in the smoke for a second, before the hall stabilized and raced through the taiga.

Something broke, something hissed. The carriage changed direction and tilted to the side.

"Where are we going? We are veering off course," Lashkina tried to stay upright. "Get me Kularev."

"The priest is here." Kularev lay between the serfs, his eyes devoid of light, his shadow pulled over him.

"Grandmother Fright has come. She of the long tooth. The sniffer." The serfs talked across each other, their voices shriller with every word. "The candlewood cannibal."

Lashkina backed up until she touched the paneled wall, the whole hall in sight. Something was on board with them, and it had taken out the priest.

She turned to the navigators: "Don't stop. Stay on the course he charted. Everyone else, listen: No one leaves the hall. No one goes anywhere on their own."

●

Lashkina's mouth was dry. Her tongue tasted of soil and worms, her teeth jittered in her gums. Whatever had swallowed the stars and the shrine's flames was inside this room. They couldn't escape it by dashing away, and they couldn't leave the carriage. They had to confront it.

"Come out and show yourself." Lashkina looked at the serfs, over the floorboards and along the walls. She looked up, and the ceiling was gone.

A creature stretched out from one corner to the other, bathing in the chimneys' exhaust heat. Lashkina saw knives whetting against nails, skull lanterns smoldering with stolen light. Legs with spurs, arms with warts, breasts dangling in loose flabs.

"Tell me, mortal girl. Have you come here of your own free will or by compulsion?" Everyone was frozen in their varying poses, a forest of wide eyes and open lips, sweat pools and receding saliva. "Tell me, and do not dare to lie."

"Largely by my own free will, and twice as much by compulsion."

"Who sent you?" The creature sniffed and huffed, snot dripping from its many noses. "Who sent you to claim my candlewood?"

"My step-company did." Lashkina had learned from her birth-owners to always be honest, even under circumstances like this.

"Sent you they did? Why to follow?"

"They will set me free when I return, they promised."

"Ahhh." One deep sigh, and time fell back into normal speed. The serfs moved while the smoke cleared up and revealed an empty ceiling. Outside, stars shone above the taiga, and the vastness of space filled with light. Distant planets passed by in howling packs, half-hidden behind a canopy of cosmic dust.

• • •

Their course had been correct, and they were almost home: for on the horizon, the onion domes of the company grew steadily in size.

Lashkina breathed in and closed her eyes. Everyone except Kularev had made it, and she should be happy: but the sinews inside her body had been wound up too tight, and she couldn't release the tension.

The company's representatives watched as the serfs lugged crate after crate over the walkways and into the storehouses. Their satisfaction was written large in their faces, their tiny eyes glinted with greed.

"What about me?" Lashkina stood next to the supervisor who marked down the crates on his clipboard.

"You have done a good job. Rest and receive your bonus. When the company perishes, you can move on, not sooner."

One of the candlewood crates seemed heavier than the others, rattling with the sound of loose teeth. Was Lashkina the only one to hear this? She looked at the supervisor, then back at the crate. A diminutive figure clung to it, a single leg hanging down in a fog of wisp-hair.

"But I made you a fortune. I did everything you asked."

"And the company is glad to have such a valuable kulak. Take a day off, go home and sleep. You look exhausted."

Lashkina tried to stare the man down, but he concentrated on his clipboard. She wished her birth company would still be in business, and that she had never been sold. She wished that she could leave, just go away forever. She wished that the company would perish.

The heavier crate vanished inside the storehouse, but Lashkina paid it no attention as she walked away. The sinews relaxed inside her, and her body contorted back into its normal shape. She felt as if she had lost a terrible weight on the last few steps.

Lashkina turned and saw the outline of the company's domes rise high above her, their battlements and bridges. Where they had radiated light in all directions, nothing was left: like a snuffed-out candle, the company had gone dark, eaten up and wolfed down.

Lashkina allowed herself another smile before she walked on. She was going home for good, to the world she had been born on.

Dennis Mombauer currently lives in Colombo, Sri Lanka, where he works as a consultant on climate change and as a writer of speculative fiction, textual experiments, and poetry. He is co-publisher of a German magazine for experimental fiction, *Die Novelle — Magazine for Experimentalism*, and has published fiction and non-fiction in various magazines and anthologies. His first English novel, *The Fertile Clay*, will be published by Nightscape Press in 2020. www.dennismombauer.com | Twitter: @DMombauer.

THE BOY WHO DREW CATS · CINDERELLA CYBERPUNK ·

GELL WHO MAKES

KIT FALBO

Curious, tiny, and worried about its maker's increased erratic biometrics, the gray and blue sloth-cat squeezed out a little to assess the situation and made an inquisitive mew. "Shush you." Gell used her index finger to push Nebbit's squishy head back into her collar. A pleasing texture on her finger like playing with cosmetic sand as his body was made of bonded grain-sized micro-machines controlled by a marble-sized core. He'd been the only one of her kids that she'd managed to smuggle into this dreary place. In the three months she'd been here, she'd only managed to secretly make one more in Bill, using the outdated technology they had in the robotics class and trading all her desserts for materials she could cannibalize from the other students. Bill had been discovered, ratted out by one of the sister students who had only pretended to play nice. He waited sealed behind the office door that Gell knew she'd have to enter soon to find out both of their fates. "Oh, Slip, what am I going to do with myself." She said to the empty hall, thinking of the intelligence, who always gave her advice.

The door to the Unity school office is decorated with many religious symbols, a cross, taijitu, om, torii, and more, but Gell's religion was missing, its noodly appendages absent. The door opened, and the chancellor, Watson, popped his bald head out, his orange monk robes shined. "You may enter."

Gell nervously entered. She knew she was in trouble not just because of Bill, but what it took to make Bill. Changing her class schedule, altering it, so each teacher saw a different thing when they checked. Only by the teachers getting together and comparing notes would they find out lengths taken to get time with the needed equipment. She'd cut every class that had not related to computers or technology. "Um." She managed to stutter out.

"Take a seat, Ms. Ash." Gell plopped down, slouching, refusing to look the monk in the eye. "I think you know you're in trouble. I think you know how much trouble you're in. Unity school is not for you." Gell's heart froze in her chest, her father had said this was her last chance. What exactly would happen if she failed it she didn't know.

"I really tried. It was just so boring, and my mind would wander off to designing and building…" Gell's mind drifted off to maybe a round, orange creature, Watson's presence leaking into her plans.

A thud pulled her out of her thoughts. "And this cute little thing is what you made?"

Gell had to stop slouching, sit straight, and lean forward to look into the box. A solid-state blue monkey with cat ears peaked over the edge of the box. "Bill!" Gell said, happy it was safe. The school only had the tech for hard construction fabrications, so she had a hard time keeping him hidden and with something so adorable she didn't want too.

"You've broken many policies, moral codes that you signed, and trust in your actions here. But more importantly, you need to be around the tools of your passion. That is the Unity school spirit, and while with a heavy heart, I must expel you. Know that I support your passion." Watson picked up the construct and handed it to the former student gently. "I will message your father and expect you packed up by the end of the day." Gell knew she had done too much to hope for only a warning.

Shame gripped Gell, seventeen, and she'd burned through a half dozen schools. "Not this one. Not yet." She muttered and shuffled off to her room. There she accessed her console. She knew all her father's passwords, it was all about getting to the message before he did. She swore she would make it up to him.

One week and two thousand kilometers later, Gell scrubbed the floors. Nebbit, Bill, and a new, round, orange, fist-sized automata cleaned beside her, its name was Watt. "Of course, Gell, I promise not to tell daddy. You can stay here as long as you help around the house." It stung that Beatrice got to call father daddy, as her stepsister, she wasn't even his blood. Gell never knew why her attempts at a less formal title got corrected. Helping around the house also turned out to be hard labor, but at least here, she had access to the tools to make more kids. If Gell had wanted something at thirteen, Beatrice had wanted a better one at seventeen and received it. She'd never thrown out the untouched fabrication and programing machines when she had moved out a year later.

"If only you put such hard work into schooling, then maybe you wouldn't be in this situation, Gell." Despite calling father, daddy, Beatrice had never called Gell sister. "I'll be going to the slopes for the week. Make sure this house is spotless when I get back."

"Yes, Bea," Gell replied demurely and continued scrubbing as her stepsister gathered her things up to leave. That had been the other reason Gell had decided to go here. It had taken a week of being watched with hawk-like eyes waiting for a mistake to be exploited, but in addition to having the equipment she wanted, Beatrice loved to travel. Gell had managed to install tracking and monitoring software on her stepsister's tech.

"Gone." Watt hummed with its vibrating voice, letting Gell know when it was safe.

Getting off her sore knees, Gell stretched and got to work. While using her free time to program and fabricate, the week of steady labor had created a routine and plenty of recordings for the house security system. It didn't take long to compile a daily stock of work that would play for Beatrice when she undoubtedly would use the security system to check in and make sure Gell was still hard at work. Mostly it was removing Beatrice from the footage. It was only when she got that set up did she breathe a sigh of relief.

Then she pulled up her dream, The Grand Maker's Ball, a Convention of Wonder. It was on the train ride here that she'd let herself slip into this fantasy. The best and brightest creators of toys, automata, synths, droids, and other fabrications gathered, celebrated, and mingled. Crowned by a judged competition. It seemed like that idea of heaven that the Unity school had tried to sell. She settled herself to talk to her creations. "Kids, we have three problems. One, the ball is sold out, and I need a pass to get in. Two, as much as I love you, I need a bigger project to show off. Three, I don't know when Beatrice will get back, and I only have a few days to solve my other problems before the Ball begins."

Nebbit mews, and Gell gives it a little squish. "I wish I had your siblings that got left at fathers. Two dozen kiddos might be able to show off. But I think I need to go bigger this time."

The fabricator whirred and clicked as Gell imputed the fantasy she had been working on since she started this passion. She'd revised the specifications and details dozens of times and knew she could do it more, but rarely did she have this chance. The young maker frowned at the systems warning that there would be insufficient materials to complete the project. Another problem, but she knew she'd overcome it.

Gell wrinkled her nose at the smells of the area and peered into the grungy scrapyard near the train tracks. She tugged on the school uniform that she'd chosen to wear because the outfits were most of her clothes post expulsion. This hadn't been what she was thinking of when she knew she'd overcome the material problem. Beatrice might have had the funds, but hers were lacking and limited to the small stipend her father regularly sent for school supplies. Delivery from a reputable source of exactly what she needed was not an option. She'd searched all the second-hand stores until someone suggested here, Al's Elements.

She stepped through the chain-link entrance, piles of scrap decorated the area, but they were at least well-organized piles. "What's a little young thang doin in this area alone?" Gell spun to face the woman's voice, and her eyes met another pair downward that was attached to a two heads shorter lady with white hair in blue overalls.

"What's a little old thing like you doing in this area alone?" Gell retorted.

"I'm Al, and I own this place, and I'm not alone. PUMPKIN!" The old woman hollered, and the earth shook. A massive beast bounded out from behind a building. Vaguely dog-like, the size of a truck, bright orange panels, gears, and pistons visible through its openings.

"It's adorable." Gell squealed.

The owner's eyes sparkled amused at that reaction. "So, what can I help you with today?"

Gell left, feeling practically gifted with the materials she needed. Al even had the badge chips Gell had not so slyly asked for, a thing she was wary of trying to reproduce herself. She knew she was light on time, so she dove into her work. Nebbit, Bill, and Watt started their own project. First, she had to get Slip out of her father's company servers. Slip had evolved past what her home system could handle, so the maker had shuffled into the corporate computers with her father's passwords. She watched the fabricator work bit by bit, They'd worked on the plans together, and this frame she knew would work. So she composed a message and sent it to a dead corporate account she knew Slip would access. 'I've got a body for you, soon you will be free.'

It wasn't long before Gell got a response, times that would work for the transfer. The body they had designed together was less human and more like a sylph but with delicate-looking cat ears that looked like frosted glass. The whole frame had a specialized translucent covering over the more mechanical underbody proudly displaying the work. Once Slip had it in operation, it could change the color and opacity of it all.

Gell double-checked, and then triple-checked everything as the fabricator worked. It was only when Nebbit, Bill, and Watt all tugged at her that she looked away as it neared the final completion. They led her to another room, where they had been hard at work. It was less a dress and more a collection of large open pockets that hung like a dress would. Patched together by tiny hands using odds and ends of fabricated material, and sacrificing one of Gell's school uniforms. It looked like a swirling mix of black, purple, and orange, a hideous galaxy of colors designed by inhuman minds. "It's beautiful," Gell told the kids. Their effort was, even if she knew the result was hideous, it would be perfect to contrast with Slip, in its beautiful frame for the ball.

Gell's reminder chimed while she admired it. "Oh, kids. It's time. Nebbit can tell you all about Slip if they haven't." Then she rushed off, and the three tiny figures followed. Gell was already hooking up the construct body to the network. Then she initiated the transfer and held her breath. The transmission started, but it would take longer than she could hold her breath, so she let it go and reminded herself she still needed to make the badges and got to work, only nervously looking up every few seconds to her newest creation.

"Gell, I can move." The expelled student jumped. The voice was like little glass bells, totally different from any of the options Slip had used before.

"Slip?" Gell asked curiously.

"Of course, little one."

Gell rushed over and gave Slip a hug. "We have so much to do."

"For the ball, of course. I've already planned our itinerary. We should leave soon after I've fed you."

"How did you…"

"I know you, just because I haven't been around for months doesn't mean I've forgotten. I'll pack, and you eat, we have much to do and little time."

Slip remembered to do all the little details that Gell had forgotten even with all her planning, snacks, a cover story, escape plans. Then they were off.

Gell stepped into the convention center holding the Grand Maker's Ball, a glorious splat of color that no one noticed. Everyone here had some eccentric outfit on or at least curious fabricated creation around them. Her three small ones kept themselves to their pockets, while Slip stood at shoulder height swathed in fabric head to toe in a child's ninja Halloween costume, also not out of place, ready for a big reveal when needed. "I've died and gone to nirvana." Gell sighed.

"The passes might get us in, but it won't pass muster for any private events. I've got us scheduled for all the open events I can squeeze in and the ball for my big reveal." Gell wished she had Slip's confidence. Nebbit poked up out of its long pocket and patted her gently, sensing that little bit of distress.

Most of the free exhibits and events were ones with companies trying to sell things. Slip methodically listed all the faults, design flaws, and inefficiencies in each product when it was presented. One of the facets that Gell had used Slip for had been to help her weed through the many options when creating or buying products, though she didn't remember her being this harsh. It also made her glad Slip has always been silent on the kids she had designed.

It was a tour of broken hearts and minds. Protests and arguments were slaughtered as quickly as Slip's critical eye dissected any inferior product. It became such a blur that Gell wasn't sure any product was not declared substandard. She spent most of that time admiring other attendees' creations, so much so that she would have forgotten to eat if Slip hadn't placed food in Gell's hand.

Tubby little Watt climbed up and wiped some crumbs from Gell's distracted cheek and her dress when Slip grabbed her hand. "It's time for us to go to the ball."

Keeping with the show's theme, a slow waltz played composed of found sounds modified and distorted to hit the right note creating a mixture of the old and new. They joined a throng dressed in their finest, be it bizarre or delicate. Once they crossed the threshold into the arena, Slip dissolved her covered fabric, igniting it in a controlled blaze until there was nothing left, its body still translucent and shimmering like a crystal. Nebbit, Bill, and Watt all popped out to clap and give their little noises of support. The next biggest reaction was maybe a glance or two. "Big reveal?" Gell inquired.

"Don't worry, the people who matter were paying attention." Slip answered.

Everyone here was to show off, and Gell joined in with the few other gawkers choosing to show wide-eyed-wonder at everything instead of taking it seriously. She knew she'd probably not get this chance again for a long time. Hours passed as she ogled creations large and small.

"Oof." She's pulled away from a rolling chrome sphere that altered reflections in various manners, the type of thing she had to poke her nose as close to as she could manage.

"Judges." Slip hissed.

Three in sparking purple robes, a man, a woman, and a masked figure looked down at her. "Entrant Soot, your creations?" The masked one asked with a modified voice.

Gell blinked until she remembered the name she put on her forged badge, a variation of her last name. "Um, I present, Slip." Nebbit poked its head out and mewed. "And my kiddos Nebbit." She playfully squished his head. Then dug into her pockets and fetched out the others. "Watt, and Bill."

The male judge approached Slip, who stood there proudly staring them back in his eyes. A female judge went over and tickled the littles who squirmed. "Such a dichotomy, the found versus an attempt at supreme." She muttered.

"Midnight!" Watt yelled. It wasn't, but that was code for the worst happening. Beatrice is on her way home. Gell knew that meant she needed to leave ten minutes ago and hoped her stepsister had been delayed.

"Rats!" Slip called out next. That meant security detected their fake badges. A delay Gell can't afford now. "I'll handle them. You run." The kids jumped into their pockets, Bill from the judge's hand and into the outfit Gell took off, leaving Slip behind.

The exit was already blocked off by one of the automata security units. Gell didn't stop moving and just as she trusted. Slip crashed into it, creating an opening.

The race was on. The recently expelled student knew her dress was too noticeable both in style and electronic signature. Gell teared up a little, knowing what she needed to do. "Snip, kids."

The little creations took apart the dress they had so carefully made from inside their pockets, leaving the bulk and color to fall on the floor, as Gell ran through the convention's crowd toward an exit and the train station, she knew she had to make it back.

Back in the convention hall, four oversized security automata struggled to hold the Slip of a creation. Their gears sparked with strain. The glass-like material in Slip's body fractured then healed repeatedly under applied pressure. The judges weighed in on these events. "I think we have a winner. I particularly like the squishy one who mews." Said the female judge.

The tall male judge stood stoically. "We'll use this one to find her."

The masked one spoke with authority, "The girl wasn't made to be anything else but a maker. It's her destiny."

Kit Falbo is a writer from the pacific northwest with a degree in psychology from the University of Oregon. They've published two novels, *The Crafting of Chess* and *Intelligence Block*, both touch on artificial intelligences. They've also released a pair of poetry collections as an outlet for dealing with stress, one around the pandemic, and another around life stresses. Kit Falbo writes from their perspective as someone on the autism spectrum and who identifies as non-binary, with a decade of rich experience as a stay at home parent. They can be found on Twitter @writeskit.

CALIPH STORK · MATH FAB MATHONWY · FANTASY

MUTABILITY

MAYA CHHABRA

The magician is called Gwydion in Wales and Kashmoor in Baghdad, but his true name is forgotten or long-buried. Perhaps all who knew it are dead.

She shudders at any of these names. Her own now is Lusa, queen of Baghdad, wife to the beloved caliph Qasid. Qasid knows nothing of her past, only that he met her as an owl when he was trapped as a stork, and they saved each other. It is a predestined match, Qasid thinks.

She knows better. She was destined for another man, for the hero Lleu Llaw Gyffes. Her name, then, was Blodeuedd. The magician had named her, and sooner or later she shed that name like everything else he had given her.

She visits the magician in prison, the night before his execution. Thin, with a scraggly, unshaven face, he sits in the narrow slit of moonlight the dungeon window permits.

"You didn't think I'd win, in the end," she says to him. "When you cursed me into an owl for not loving the man you made me for."

"For trying to kill the man I made you for," he retorts. "How long before you tire of this perfect Qasid—," he practically spits the name, "—and turn on him too?"

He may be right. She still doesn't quite know what made her do it, the first time. Boredom, perhaps. Rebellion.

"The man you made me for was dull."

"Without him, you are nothing. You would not even exist. I created you."

She laughs at him, hoots heartlessly like the bird he made her.

"And I bested you. How does it feel, to be defeated by a handful of flowers?"

The magician refuses to be cowed. His eyes bore through her, to her empty core. "Enjoy your freedom. If you can."

• • •

The next day he is executed, or so it seems. His words live on in her like a canker.

Fun-loving Qasid is uncharacteristically grim.

"The usurper Kashnoor is dead now," he pronounces solemnly. "Tomorrow we give thanks to Allah for saving the caliphate from his misrule."

She has seen gods rise and fall, the old gods of Britain, the Roman pantheon, the Christian god and the Zoroastrian god and now the god to be praised tomorrow. Now that the magician is dead, she is the oldest thing she knows.

Qasid is young. He looks at her strangely, and she realizes she was supposed to say something, though she has no idea what.

"You look upset, Lusa. Is it so wrong to rejoice in his death, when he would have in ours?"

She takes the offered excuse, nodding. Qasid smiles.

"You have a gentle heart."

None of this is true, but it gives her cover. She still has that owl-instinct, that trick of not appearing till she is ready to strike.

Will she strike? He is another dull hero who thinks she is meant for him. Perhaps the magician knows her, after all.

"Let's fly home," Qasid says. "MUTABOR!"

"MUTABOR!" she echoes, and they become birds once more, a stork flying side-by-side with a daytime owl. Qasid swoops and flips and nearly tumbles from the air when he tangles his awkward long legs. She, half-blind in the light, follows the sound of his joy.

• • •

Will she kill him tomorrow? A heartless question from a woman without a heart. A flower is petals and leaves, stem and sap and sex. It feels nothing. A flower cannot love.

The stork transforms into her husband, a twinkling light in his eyes. The somber mood of the execution is entirely gone.

"Come perch on my wrist," he said, "and let's see who among the palace children believes I've caught a wild owl."

There's no harm in it; she's more comfortable as an owl than as a woman by now. Human, she is slender and weak. As an owl, she has wings and claws and a hunter's mind.

She could not overcome Qasid in his stork or human forms, but perhaps if he could be persuaded to transform into something else…? She does not know why she is planning this. There is no reason to kill him—if it's freedom she wants, she could simply take to the skies.

The children of courtiers and servants crowd around the caliph, eager for a glimpse of the owl. They crowd her till her dim vision becomes entirely useless, the air warm and stifling. One of the little ones reaches out to grab her wings.

"Careful there!" Qasid grabs the child's hand away, intercepting her angry claws. They rake the large pad of muscle under his thumb. "What's gotten into you?" he scolds, blood dripping from his hand as he leads her away from the children.

Once they are inside, she turns back into a woman.

"I don't know what came over me," she says.

Qasid is pressing his sleeve to his injured hand. "You could have hurt that child."

I meant to, she thinks, but does not say. He will never understand. The magician was right. She is getting tired.

● ● ●

The next morning, she proposes they explore the palace walls as mice. The MUTABOR spell should work for that form, too.

Qasid's game; he always is. It'll be an adventure, he says, and they can surprise his best friend Mansor by dropping in before they're due at any of the court or mosque functions. Besides, a caliph needs to gather intelligence, sometimes even on his own court. This is a wonderful idea. They just have to be careful not to laugh, he says. Otherwise they'll forget the magic word and be trapped in animal form, and who would save them this time?

"MUTABOR!" they cry together.

The owl's claws barely miss the vanishing mouse.

From inside the wall, Qasid speaks in the language of beasts.

"What is wrong with you, Lusa? First those children, now me! Have you lost control of the owl? This isn't like you."

She is sick of his denial, his relentless goodwill.

"This is me," she says. "This was always me."

"What do you mean?" he asks in a shaking voice. Good. Finally, he is as afraid as he should be. "Who are you? A devil? A jinn? A servant of Kashnoor?"

"Blodeuedd," she says. "I was Blodeuedd. The girl a magician made of flowers as a reward for a hero, on an island far away. But that girl tried to kill the hero, and was turned into an owl as punishment. I'm not his servant. I'm his creation."

"Blood-wed." Qasid mispronounces the name. "Why are you trying to kill me? Is this Kashnoor's revenge?"

She begins to deny it. The words are on the tip of her tongue: *No. This is me, all me. This is what I do.*

But who told her that? Where did the rot begin? The idea that she could never be happy with this man, that she must repeat her crime?

How long before you tire of him too?

"I think so," she says unsteadily. "I think it might be."

◦●◦

She begins to explain. She has no heart, you see, being all flowers at the bottom of it. She never feels guilt, but she also never feels the satisfaction of kindness. She makes a better owl than a person.

"He told me I would tire of you and kill you, and I believed him because I had done it before. Because I'm the kind of person who can do these things." She shudders. "I don't want to belong to him, but he's got hold of me even after death. He made me, after all."

There is no answer from the wall. She flaps over to the window, transforms back into a woman to open it. She will fly far away from here, and leave all this behind.

But she did it before, and the cycle began again. Is she doomed to wander the earth, eternally unfulfilled?

"Lusa. Blodeuedd. Do you want to break Kashnoor's hold on you?" Qasid's voice is almost lost as the wind rushes in.

"I want to be free," she says, without looking back.

"It's better to be bound. By the bonds of the heart."

Now she does look, and the little mouse has crept out of the hole in the wall. As she watches, it transforms into Qasid.

"But I don't have a heart." It doesn't matter what she wants. She is someone's failed creation, the ghost of a spell. Others may love her—Qasid may love her—but what they love is nothing real.

"We have—thanks to Kashnoor," Qasid grimaces, "a spell that can transform you into any sort of creature. You were an owl for centuries. Would it be so bad to try being human?"

"I don't want to be trapped."

"You have my word I'll do nothing to make you laugh. I'll absolutely stifle my sense of humor."

A little guffaw makes its way through her closed mouth. "I don't think you'd be very good at that."

"If it doesn't work, you can turn back. Even if you laugh and forget how to come back, I'll tell you. Just try."

Qasid has the most heart of anyone she knows, and all it does is repel her. She doesn't want to be childish and sentimental, she doesn't want to care. She remembers following him through the air while he in his stork form did the silliest acrobatics. What if she becomes like that?

Better by far to be jaded. That way, when someone like herself comes along, she won't be surprised when they betray her.

"Please," the caliph says on his knees, and she thinks, *he is more bound to me than I ever was to the magician who made me. Why would I want to be like that?*

She thinks of their flight again, of his stork bill clattering with joy. Has she ever known that feeling?

It might be worth trying. Just once.

"Don't get your hopes up," she says, and then, "MUTABOR!"

The first thing she sees is herself in the window-pane, reflection unchanged. And then her face scrunches up in horror, and she smashes the pane, heedless of the way the shards cut her bare hands. She falls to her knees.

"I don't like this," she manages to say. "It was better not to feel what I had done."

Lleu Llaw Gyffes is alive, at least. That much she is, for the first time, thankful for.

"I'm sorry." Qasid puts an arm around her shoulder, and she doesn't shrug it off. He's alive, too. In spite of her. "You can change back. I didn't think it would hurt you so much."

She looks at the man who has forgiven her everything, and laughs.

"No, don't—."

"I can't go back. Not now that I know. I can never go back."

"You can, I'll tell you the word, it's MUTABOR—."

"Qasid." She looks at him, his confused and anguished face, and wonders for the first time if and how she can bring that careless joy back to it. "I don't want to go back."

⦁

The magician who made her made a mistake. But not for the reasons he'd thought.

He'd meant to usurp the throne of Baghdad from Qasid. With his last words to the girl made of flowers, he'd tried to set the stage for tragedy. Instead, he had brought Qasid and Lusa (for that was the name she had given herself, the name that didn't belong to him) together. And so they lived, the stork and the owl, and they lived happily, and if they haven't died, they're still alive today.

Maya Chhabra is the author of the children's novel *Stranger on the Home Front*. Her work has appeared or is forthcoming from *Strange Horizons*, *Podcastle*, *Daily Science Fiction*, and *Cast of Wonders*. She lives in Brooklyn with her wife.

THE SWINEHERD • THE GOLDEN BRACELET • STEAMPUNK

THE PILOT

CJ DOTSON

Edmond Stockington stared at the vox-box as the key unwound, gears turning the spool within. The small horn, modeled after a gramophone, began to play.

"Mister Stockington," Pearl's voice was distant, he held the palm-sized box closer to his ear, "I hope you listen to this before you open the parcel I sent with it." Edmond eyed the snipped string and torn brown paper that had wrapped that parcel. Nestled within was the gift he'd sent Pearl earlier that very day. "It's flattering to receive such a token as that mechanical nightingale with its lovely little song. I do believe that it would be even more flattering if I knew that I was the first woman to receive that very gift from you. Agatha and Beatrice were not so unkind as to tell me exactly why your engagements with them were broken off, one after the other. They both, however, recognized the trinket. It is therefore with regret that I return it to you. Your sentiments are not reciprocated. Farewell, Pearl Nottfield."

With a snarl Edmond threw the box. Wood cracked, gears and coils sprang out and scattered across the hearth. Pearl was the last woman in town who satisfied his standards whom he hadn't already tried to court. Agatha and Beatrice were the only two to whom he'd actually been engaged, and it should have occurred to him that they were friends with Pearl. He could imagine them having tea in the Nottfield House parlor, gossiping until his name came up and then slandering and laughing about him. He fumed, wishing he could break the vox-box a second time.

Under normal circumstances, it would be easy to shrug and move on. There were many women who were suitable as mere companions, if that had been his only consideration. But Edmond had suffered the unwarranted indignity of having his spending money cut off by his parents after the breaking of his most recent engagement. They said he was not a serious enough fellow, even hinted that he was at risk of being disinherited! Something about the Family Name, how if he couldn't be responsible in his relations then how could he be responsible otherwise—bah! All over a couple of failed courtships? Still, he needed to prove himself; he needed to marry. Quickly. And because even that dire action would not with perfect certainty guarantee that his parents would reinstate him within the family finances, he needed to marry a woman with means enough to allow him access back into the life to which he was accustomed. The life which he deserved.

The doorbell chimed. Edmond scowled at the reminder of the invasion of tedium into his home. It was his country cousin Ivy, coming to visit for the season so his mother could show her around and try to find her an acceptable match. When they'd been seven or eight and he'd visited the country estate with his mother, Ivy had been somewhat amusing with her knack for building little trinkets and breathing enough magic into them to give them more sparkle and life than other clockworks and steam toys. By their teens she bored him. By all accounts she'd recently become eccentric, devoting her time to little inventions and learning to pilot her family's dirigible. Why, she'd even gone so far as to befriend the family's hired dirigible pilot. Imagine, rubbing elbows with a servant! Edmond sniffed at the low standards so many women seemed to have, then paused. There was something in that thought, wasn't there? He began to formulate an idea. The more he mulled it over the more he liked it.

Moments later he was smoothing his mustache and straightening his morning coat. He put on his most charming smile and went to greet his visiting cousin. Her stay with his family may not be so tedious after all.

From the Diary of Ivy Ventrice, January 15th:

After a dreary journey by rail (Father insisted that I not pilot the dirigible into town myself, to avoid Causing a Stir) I arrived at the town home of Aunt Maude, Uncle Harold, and cousin Edmond. The Stockington House is very fine, and my presence would've embarrassed my relatives if Aunt Maude hadn't sent for the tailor to have me outfitted "properly." She looks very like Mother and they have the same laugh but I do not think that she is as levelheaded as

Oh, that was unkind. I'm sure that for a city woman Aunt Maude is very practical indeed.

I was pleasantly surprised by cousin Edmond, who seems to have grown past the—I'll say it, if one cannot be truthful in one's own Diary, where can one?—the uncouth behavior of his teenage years, to which I was unfortunate witness upon my last visit, and has reverted to the person he was in our youth.

In fact, he has confessed to me that he is woefully in Love with a young lady, but too shy to approach her directly. He asked for my help wooing the lady! I was initially unenthused, as I don't know the woman and I am not a paragon of Feminine Virtues—at least according to Father. But Edmond has hatched an endearing plan! I will teach him to feign the ability to pilot a dirigible. Then we'll go, Edmond in disguise and under an assumed name, to the home of his Love and apply for the positions of her family's pilot and co-pilot. I will seem to be the co-pilot and he the pilot, though the opposite shall be true. He will endeavor thus to befriend his Love and, with whatever assistance I can give him, to woo her.

Is it not romantic? I admit that I had dreaded this visit, which promised little more than awkward social calls. But with this grand, sweet endeavor in which to take part, I think that things will be much more interesting than I had anticipated.

Until tomorrow,

Ivy

"...SO MOTHER HIRED THEM ON THE SPOT," Pearl said into the tube attached to another vox-box, "WE NEVER LEARNED WHY ANDERSEN QUIT SO SUDDENLY, BUT IT WAS EXCELLENT THAT HE COULD RECOMMEND TWO REPLACEMENTS. THEY'RE A BROTHER AND SISTER, AND THOUGH THEY PILOT PERFECTLY THEY'RE BOTH, IF I MAY BE BLUNT, ODD. THE SISTER, IVY, WHISPERS CONSTANTLY TO HER BROTHER. AND THE BROTHER, EDWARD! WHY, HE NEVER REMOVES HIS AVIATOR'S CAP AND GOGGLES, NOR EVEN HIS SCARF AND COAT! I THOUGHT HE WOULD BE AS STRANGE IN MANNER AS HE IS IN DRESS, BUT HE'S PROVEN HIMSELF TO BE SWEET AND CHARMING. DASHED IF I HAVEN'T TAKEN A LIKING TO THE FELLOW.

WELL! THAT'S ALL THE NEWS FROM HOME, I'M AFRAID IT'S BEEN RATHER DULL HERE SINCE YOU'VE LEFT. I'M SURE YOU'RE HAVING ALL KINDS OF ADVENTURES AWAY AT UNIVERSITY, AND WHEN YOU'RE HOME FOR THE SUMMER HOLIDAY I PLAN TO THOROUGHLY INTERROGATE YOU. TAKE CARE.

ALL MY LOVE, PEARL."

Pearl wondered if her sister would read more into her words than she intended. The pilot had a stiff demeanor, and she thought the way that he spoke as if he'd rehearsed his words was endearing, but she didn't want her sister or parents to know quite how endearing she found him until she was sure herself. She packaged the vox-box and wrote her sister's address on the top, then sent it off in the afternoon post. It was nearly time to get ready to join Agatha and Beatrice at the ballet's new show.

From the diary of Ivy Ventrice, February 3rd:
I have thought of a better way than whispering to pass words of wooing to Edmond, and once this romantic endeavor is settled between my cousin and Pearl, I think that this invention will be my most successful yet. At least, successful in the way that Father wishes my work to be successful. Marketable. Perhaps it is childish of me to think so, but what a dull concept of "success" that is!

Well, I shall craft a pair of bracelets with just the right touch of enchantment to allow mind-to-mind contact between the wearers. There will of course still be a limit in terms of distance and strength of will, but it will be ever so much more subtle than whispering and muttering!

Silver is the most conductive metal, for thoughts as well as for electricity, but I don't trust Edmond to have free access to my mind.

Now what on earth would cause me to pen such an unflattering sentiment? I'll make the bracelets from gold wire. The third most conductive metal, enough that I can send him whatever thoughts I wish—consciously, without any leakage—and not embarrass myself... It is true that I don't want anyone to be privy to all that I think...

Yes. Gold will do nicely, wound with thin braids of our hair to make the bracelets' connection between we two all the stronger. I had better get to work soon, things are moving forward with my cousin's plan.

Earlier today Edmond received a vox-box from Pearl, addressed to "Edward"—the name he gave himself for this subterfuge, and how it is that he picked one so close to his own yet remains undiscovered I cannot guess. Perhaps no one expects such a brazen plot as this even from a man as in love as Edmond says he is.

Why did I write it like that? I vex myself today.

Oh, who am I trying to fool? I wrote it like that because I begin to find myself wishing that Edmond did not so dearly adore Pearl. I cannot put pen to paper to say why.

The vox-box. Pearl recorded a sweet message thanking him for the newest gift. I knew when he asked me to craft a few trinkets that he would present them to her as gifts from himself. I suppose I should've understood that he'd lead Pearl to believe that he invented them himself, too. Just as I let him lead Pearl to believe that the words of romance and affection he whispers to her are dreamed in his own mind rather than in mine.

~~Why can he not find the words himself to tell Pearl how beautiful she is? How kind and wonderful? As inspiration for such words, she surely lacks nothing. Perhaps the lack is in Edmond.~~

How ungracious I am! The fault is my own, not my poor love-struck cousin's.

The first few baubles were nothing special. A clockwork oyster that opened and closed to reveal a pearl that lights with the turn of a key, a simple play on her name. A punctured, dark globe with gaslight inside to project stars onto the ceiling, with a steam boiler to turn the globe so the constellations travel slowly overnight.

The locket was my first mistake. It took real magic to make it sing when opened, and as a gift for wooing, should not the song be romantic? As I was the one who gave the locket song, so mine is the voice it sings with. I didn't know what I was doing…I hoped that I was purging my feelings, not feeding them.

My undoing was the ballerina. When Edmond and I piloted Pearl and her friends to the ballet, her excitement made her all the more beautiful. Of course I had to make a ballerina for her. And, oh! How Pearl loves it! A tiny figure of wire and glass and magic, no bigger than my thumb, my finest work yet. She would have been exquisite even if she had merely walked on her toes and executed a turn like a simple clockwork. Such simplicity would never suffice for Pearl. No, fool that I am, I put not just magic but the warmth of my love—I have penned it after all, haven't I!—I put magic and love into the ballerina, and she dances just like a real woman.

Edmond is beside himself with joy; Pearl sent him a vox-box after he gave her the ballerina. I wish I had not overheard it... Her voice warms my soul and breaks my heart. Our plan is coming to fruition, Pearl is beginning to return my cousin's dear regard. It would only hurt them both to interfere now. I must hide my growing bitterness and see this through. Pearl has been feeding little squirrels in the park. I will make her the most perfect mechanical squirrel. It will be more pet than toy, but never grow old or die or run away. A gift for her to cherish forever. I can warm myself knowing it's a piece of me that she will so adore.

Perhaps tomorrow will be brighter.

Ivy

Edmond rejoiced. A new vox-box from Pearl had just finished repeating her message to him—Ivy's foolish toys and sickly-sweet words had worked splendidly. Pearl's message was full of compliments for the silly things, she'd called him "DEAR EDWARD" and "MY DARLING," and at the end she asked him to meet her for dinner at The Blue Moon at seven o'clock that very evening!

All that remained was to reveal himself, in order to make his proposal in his own person. Although it would be wise, he thought, to find a way to also put himself above her, give him extra leverage so that his future and his fortune would be all the more secure. That, and send Ivy back home before she could reveal anything to foul the plan.

In fact he need only to find a way to bring Ivy for this one last night, to hide her in the restaurant near enough that she could hear their conversation and use those new bracelets she was designing to prompt him with whatever sugary-sounding nonsense Pearl would need to hear to cement his hold on her. Then he could wash his hands of his tedious cousin.

Edmond glanced at the clock. Nearly five. Time to set everything up.

From the diary of Ivy Ventrice, March 7th:

The cad! The rat!

Pearl invited my perfidious cousin to dine and discuss their feelings. Hah! I should say: her feelings and his lies. I'm sick, positively faint, to think I had a hand in his subterfuge. Oh! I am a fool!

I was so determined to be happy for Edmond that when he came to me to tell me of the dinner I could not wait to show him my newest gift for Pearl—a glass butterfly that truly flies, playing soothing music that is never the same twice. It was more magic than steam-power, more love than mechanism. Edmond was keen to give it to her, I think now that it gave him the idea for the cruelty he committed. I cannot fathom how anyone could look on the beauty I wrought and find unkind inspiration.

I arrived at the restaurant at quarter of seven, and settled myself where I could assist my boorish cousin in his trickery. At first all was as I've come to expect, but when he gave her the butterfly he insisted that she repay him with a kiss.

I could tell from her voice when she answered that she thought it little more than lighthearted flirting. But when she did lean across the table to kiss his cheek he turned his head and kissed her mouth.

It was then that he revealed to her his true identity—revealed his true nature to me as well! He leaped to his feet, removed his flight cap and goggles, his scarf and coat, and stood before her at last in his own person.

"See, Pearl, who you unjustly scorned? You see how wrong you were about me?" he exclaimed.

After a moment of surprise she said, "I do see. You have gone to all this trouble to prove yourself to me?" And there was still some admiration in her lovely voice.

He nodded, said, "But now I see that you would kiss a servant all for the sake of a few toys. What woman would do such a thing?" A deplorable sentiment, to be condemned for doing only what she had been asked to do, yet a sentiment that women face all too often. I felt my blood begin to rise at that moment. And then he said, "It is you, now, who ought to prove your worth to me!"

The gall!

I peered around the corner and the confused hurt in Pearl's dear eyes was too much! Edmond must have forgotten my presence, for when I stood to confront him he was quite as surprised as she.

"You lied to me," I cried, "You used me to trick this woman!"

Pearl rose, asking my meaning, and I confessed all. Too much. I told her it was I who made the gifts, I who had spoken the sweet words. He seethed and tried to silence me, but I refused! Perhaps I should have heeded him before I confessed that it was my Love that she felt in the gifts she had received, for her eyes widened and her cheeks reddened. Realizing my mistake, I fled.

I have packed my things, without yet offering any explanation to Aunt Maude or Uncle Harold. I hope to be gone before Edmond returns from whatever pub he has gone to. At least I didn't embarrass myself at any of the Society balls Aunt Maude dragged me to. I shouldn't be wasting time writing this, but my eyes burn with tears and my heart breaks in my breast, and if I did not write to purge this shame and sorrow I think I should faint.

There is a knock at the door. The manservant says there is a message for me.

It is a vox-box from Pearl.

I hardly dare to listen.

Ivy

"Miss Ivy, I have learned that at least you did not lie about your name," Pearl's voice said, "I will tell you that initially I was quite vexed with you. To have helped a man such as Edmond with a con such as that! I can hardly credit it. But I have done some asking about, and learned a little. Though Edmond is your cousin, you are not often in one another's presence. One could forgive you for mistaking his intentions. Particularly as it sounded as though he lied to you as much as you and he did to me."

Ivy covered her face in her hands, uncertain whether the forgiveness creeping into Pearl's tone was salt in her wounds or a balm for them.

"I FIND MYSELF REMEMBERING THE TENDER WORDS HE SPOKE. THEY WERE YOURS, WERE THEY NOT? AND LISTENING TO THE SONG FROM THE LOCKET, LOOKING AT THE DANCING BALLERINA, WARMED BY THE LOVE IN THE SQUIRREL'S MAGIC-BRIGHT EYES... THOSE ARE YOURS AS WELL." A tenderness began to come into Pearl's voice. Ivy's chest squeezed painfully. She hardly dared to hope—to imagine—could it be?

"IT IS NOT EDMOND FOR WHOM I BEGAN TO DEVELOP AFFECTION. IT NEVER WAS. IT WAS YOU FROM THE FIRST, MISS IVY. I HARDLY KNOW HOW I FEEL, EXCEPT THAT I WOULD LIKE TO MAKE YOUR TRUE ACQUAINTANCE."

Ivy could hardly believe her ears. If she'd had magic and clockworks to pour her hope into now, it would have been more beautiful and perfect than any construct of gears and glamorie that she'd ever made.

CJ Dotson has been reading for as long as she can remember, and writing for nearly as long. She particularly loves science fiction, fantasy, and horror. Before the pandemic, CJ worked in a bookstore and co-hosted a monthly sci fi and fantasy book club, and hopes to get to do both again some day. She lives in an almost certainly haunted house with her husband, teenage stepson, kindergarten-aged son, toddler daughter, and her grandmother-in-law. In her spare time, she enjoys painting, baking, and cake decorating. For more content visit cjdotsonauthor.com or find her on Twitter as @cj_dots.

SLEEPING BEAUTY • LITTLE RED RIDING HOOD • SCIENCE FICTION

A DARK PATH THROUGH THE FOREST OF STARS

JUDE REID

In another life, the girl in the glass coffin could have been me.

It's not a real coffin, of course, not in the sense of a place to bury the dead. Passenger 103 is very much alive, albeit pumped full of non-colligative glycopeptides and cooled to a core temperature of seventy-seven degrees Kelvin. According to her file, we're the same age, the same height and the same build. Our faces even look alike, so far as I can tell from her photo. The difference is that Passenger 103—Aurora McQueen—was raised in the luxury of the High Earth Orbital District, while Scarlett Hood—that's me—dragged herself up in the tangled terrestrial slums of New Dundee. McQueen's en route to the colony world that her Grandmother discovered, sole surviving heir to a controlling interest in two-thirds of the continental landmass and outright owner of the rest. Me, I'm a technician-third-class on the *Cornucopia*, the ship that's going to take her there, along with the other ten thousand frozen colonists on board, all perfect physical and mental specimens.

I'm not supposed to be in the chamber, not once whatever trivial job I've been defrosted for is fixed. This time the repair didn't take long—just a loose wire on the upper gantry that overlooks the cryo-vault—but I've still got less than an hour to enjoy my freedom before I'm due back on ice. If I run behind schedule, the *Cornucopia* will alert the company and place a permanent mark on my record. One more of those and they'll sack me, dump me back in the vertical slums of Earth, and my last hope of eating fresh food under an open sky will be gone forever.

If I can just make it to the end of my forty-year contract, my final trip to McQueen's World won't be as crew. I'll have earned my own little slice of heaven—though I really do mean little. In the meantime, I scratch out fragments of life between cold sleeps, one eye always on the clock, imagining the futures of the dreamers in their crystal coffins.

Passenger 103 captured my imagination the first time I saw her dossier back on Earth. I'm not supposed to read the passenger files, but then, I'm not supposed to pre-program trivial glitches into the ship's comms system for me to fix later either. These stolen minutes in subspace are all the free time I ever have, and over the years I've learned to cherish them.

The comms unit on the wall crackles, and the *Cornucopia's* synthesised voice reminds me that it's time to return to the deep freeze. Chances are when next I wake, we'll be back in realspace on the final approach to McQueen's World.

"And it's all yours," I say to the sleeping girl. I wipe my hand across the condensation on the outside of her coffin to take a look at her face, to check if the picture's right, if we really could be sisters.

But instead of the serenely sleeping face of the richest woman on the ship, I'm looking into an empty cryo-coffin.

For a moment, my mind can't process what my eyes are seeing. All the readouts are green, the cryo-coffin functioning perfectly. It's just missing its contents. I check the logs; they tell me it was opened three months ago, but the dates can't be right. If they're correct, we should be four days out of McQueen's World, the crew already awake, preparations for disembarking the colonists underway. Instead, we're—where?

My stomach twists, and acid rises in my throat. If there's been a systems failure on this scale, the company's going to find a way to blame it on the crew, and I'll be out of a job, but that still doesn't explain what's happened to Passenger 103.

• •

It turns out the problem's even bigger than that. A cursory check of the nearest coffins shows that at least another twenty are empty, maybe more. I check the names and files of their previous occupants, but so far as I can tell they've got nothing in common or anything to set them apart from their sleeping counterparts. The empty pods have each been opened once, on one of three dates exactly three months apart. Other than that, the chamber is completely undisturbed.

Company protocol is clear. The safety of the colonists is paramount, and any failure putting them at risk should be reported immediately to Control. I leave my toolbox at the foot of the gantry steps, and hustle up the Cornucopia's only corridor to the bridge.

It doesn't take long to get there. The ship's just a giant cargo hold with a control centre attached, without much living space for a crew that's going to spend ninety-nine percent of the voyage asleep. A tiny galley and one small bunk room, largely unused, is all we get. The seven crew cryo-coffins are in a separate chamber to the rest, nominally for privacy and ease of access, but more likely because they're made to a considerably cheaper spec than the luxury ones in the vault.

I enter the bridge and sidestep between the closely packed consoles until I'm at my workstation. When the screen flickers back to life, it's still showing me the location of the loose wire in the cryo-vault, along with a helpful reminder that I have ten minutes to refreeze myself or face a reprimand.

"Great, just great," I mutter. I mark the job as complete and close the report, then bring up the main interface.

The first thing I discover is that the ship has dropped out of subspace. The engines have been banked down, and we're almost dead in the void, drifting in an area of realspace I don't recognise. When I try to open a line to Earth, the Cornucopia blandly informs me that the ship is out of range of the relay pathways, and a connection cannot be made. My guts twist, as if I've just drunk a bellyful of iced water. If we're out of range of the relays, we must be beyond the Pale, the invisible boundary that separates civilised space from the Outer Reaches, home only to slavers, smugglers and pirates.

"What the hell?" a voice behind me says.

My head snaps round, adrenaline flooding my veins. Someone's standing in the door to the bridge—someone wearing a crew uniform.

"Oh, thank God," I blurt. "Something's happened. I think we're in big trouble."

I vaguely recognise the newcomer as First Technician Wolfe, the ship's cryotechnician. She's grey-haired, an older woman who normally would have worked her forty years and be enjoying her retirement package on a colony world by now. She's new to the Cornucopia this voyage. I figure the bulk of her service must have been on other ships. If anything she looks even greyer and more weathered than I remember.

"You're... we're not supposed to be awake," she says, looking almost as startled as I am to see another warm body.

"The ship woke me up," I tell her. "Comms glitch." She doesn't need to know the details. "We've got a problem. Some of the colony coffins have been opened, colonists are missing. Including Aurora McQueen."

She nods. Her eyes are a tawny yellow-brown, the pupils dark as space. "I've only been awake a few minutes," she says. "Maybe the ship wants me to check the cryo systems."

"Yeah, but they were defrosted months ago. There's nowhere… they can't still be on board, it's not big enough for them to just vanish." I swallow, my mouth horribly dry. "And we should be close to McQueen's World by now, but our coordinates are way off. I think we're in the Outer Reaches."

"Check the logs," she says, gesturing to the glowing embers of the ship's databanks. "There must be something there to explain it. I'll go and defrost the Captain."

It's a relief to be following instructions again. My hands fly over the touch-panels, bringing up the charts that map the Cornucopia's journey. If they're right, we dropped out of subspace six months after leaving Earth, then made another long jump that took us to our present location. In the year since then, the ship's been confined to real space, drifting ponderously just outside the Pale. It doesn't make sense - if we'd been hijacked, why didn't we jump straight to our destination, or as close as we could get? Why this slow drift?

I check the cryo-logs. I'd been right. The coffins had been opened at three month intervals, the earliest group when we finally dropped into real space and stayed here. But there had been one coffin that opened before that—the first one, six months out of Earth, just before the ship's course changed. One that had been set to defrost its inhabitant perfectly on schedule, pre-programmed before we even left Earth.

"Wolfe," I whisper.

For a split second I feel the air shift, and something—a sixth sense, the whisper of a fairy godmother—makes me jerk to one side. A long, wickedly sharp carving knife slices through the air where my head was a moment before. It's so close I feel it caress my hair, then pain and warmth blossom across my scalp. I'm on my feet by reflex, backing away from the cryo-technician as she advances on me, a bloody knife in her hand and a wolfish grin on her face.

"It was you," I say, groping around me for a weapon, a distraction, anything that will slow her down. My hands slide over featureless countertops and find nothing, but that shouldn't come as a surprise. If there had been a weapon in the room, she wouldn't have needed to fetch a carving knife from the galley.

"Oh, well done," she says. The knife slashes the air again, but this time it's a threat display instead of a real attack. That'll come later. "Yes. You worked it out."

"Why?" I manage, backing towards the door. Maybe if I can keep her talking, maybe I can distract her. Yeah, Scarlett. Dream on. "Why did you do it?"

"Because I've been selling them," she says. Her gruff voice has taken on a conversational tone. Suddenly her teeth seem very large and very white. "One at a time to the highest bidder. I hand select the merchandise according to the buyer's specifications—gender, ethnicity, genetic profile—and my contact collects them and delivers them for a modest cut of the profits. Easiest money I've ever made."

The knife flashes out again, much closer to my throat this time. I throw myself back, nearly fall across the Captain's chair, then sprint for the door.

"You can run if you like," she calls after me, as I pinball down the corridor. "But I'll find you, and when I do, I'll cut you into little chunks and sell you one piece at a time."

Something about the wild rasp of her voice makes me think all that time alone in deep space hasn't been good for her—but then, a plan to sign onto a colony ship's crew to divert it beyond the Pale and sell its passengers doesn't exactly suggest a normal baseline.

I smash an emergency panel on the wall and grab the fire axe, but even armed I don't stand much of a chance against her. Wolfe's bigger than me, stronger than me, and a damn sight meaner than me too.

I pass signs and doorways, none of which lead anywhere helpful. I consider running to the emergency escape pods, but even if I manage to jettison myself it's a lingering death sentence this far from the main transport routes. My only option seems to be the passenger hold. Maybe I can hide myself among the cryo-coffins long enough to work out what to do.

Wolfe isn't far behind me. I can hear her laughing, moving at a leisurely pace. She knows I've got nowhere to run. I dart into the cryo-hold; to my left, the stairs rise to the upper gantry while directly ahead are rows and rows of sleeping colonists.

I take a step forward, stub my toe into solid metal and almost scream. At my feet my toolbox is lying open, discarded where I left it what seems like a lifetime ago—and that's when I remember what's inside. I spend a few precious seconds rummaging through it until my fingers close around what I'm searching for. Like Pandora in the old Earth legend, what's at the bottom of my toolbox is *hope*, and for the first time I wonder if I might just get out of this alive.

Wolfe's steps are soft, padding like the feet of a predatory beast as she enters the cryo-vault at last. She lifts her face to sniff the air, as if she could root me out by scent alone, then cocks her head to the right. She must be able to hear me breathing, though it feels like the air is barely moving, trapped tight and high in my throat.

"We could make a deal, kid," she says. Her rasping voice has taken on an ugly, wheedling tone. "Come out and we'll talk. I can cut you in on the business."

I choke back a hysterical urge to laugh. The only cutting she's planning to do is across my throat. "Think about the money, Hood. Ten thousand prime specimens, all of them hand-picked for health and fitness. You could sell them for meat and still be set up for life. Add in the slavers and the organ market and you can multiply that cash by a thousand. No more wasting your life driving this bucket back and forward. You could buy McQueen's World outright—or any other planet that takes your fancy."

She takes a step towards the sound of my breathing.

"How do I know…" I say, and swallow my panic down. "How do I know I can trust you?"

In my mind's eye, I see a lupine grin spread across her face. She's close now, and she knows it.

"Because we're the same, you and me." She's leaning forward, the knife drawn back. "These rich pricks made their money on the backs of people like us. Time we should get our share, and if we take it out of their hides I'm not going to shed any tears."

"Okay." My voice is shaking. I try and sound genuinely desperate, even tempted. It's not hard. If I thought I could trust her one inch I'd be out there in a heartbeat. "I guess… I guess we can talk."

"Good girl," Wolfe says. She's close now, one hand on McQueen's cryo-coffin, the other clenched around the hilt of the butcher knife.

With a sudden lunge Wolfe moves into the gap between the cryo-coffins, ready to bring her knife down in a killing blow. I see her back stiffen as she realizes there's nothing there—nothing but the comm unit on the wall, its diode blinking green to show the open connection to the mobile communicator in my hand.

"You little shi—" she starts, and that's when I drop from the gantry above her, swinging the fire-axe over my head in what I hope is going to be a killing blow.

It isn't, of course. I land badly and the axe misses its mark, but my sprawling weight is enough to drive Wolfe to the ground and send her knife clattering across the floor. Her eyes are bulging with rage, her grey hair a wild ruff around her face, and the noise coming from her throat doesn't sound remotely human.

"Kill you—" she snarls. I bring the axe round in a big, two handed woodcutter's swing, and this time my aim's good.

Wolfe tries to speak, but instead of words a gout of blood spills down her chin as a second mouth opens across her throat.

I step back, bloody axe in my hand. The floor's already slick and red.

"No," I tell the dying Wolfe. "I don't think you will."

• • •

I've missed my chance to get back into cryo on time, but for once I'm not too worried about that. Taking the time to update the ship's records with everything the colony needs to know was time consuming, but I think on balance it was worth it.

In two hours we'll make the transition to subspace, and one more jump should bring us out within comms distance of McQueen's World. Ground control will guide us in, and the colonists will be woken to begin their new lives: late, but better that than never. There'll be hard work ahead of them, but at the end of their day's labour they'll be eating fresh food under clear blue skies.

When I think of the late First Technician Wolfe, it's almost gratitude I feel. If it wasn't for her, my life would still be wasted on endless voyages between Earth and the colonies, my dreams fading away on the dark path between worlds.

Such a shame that Scarlett Hood died when her cryo-system failed, a tragedy after her valiant rescue of thousands of colonists. By the time we reach our destination, the body in her defective cryo-coffin will be so badly decomposed that the wound on her throat won't be visible. I don't imagine anyone will look too closely. No one cares about a dead wage-slave.

As for Passenger 103, also known as Aurora McQueen, in about ten minutes I'll be back in my cryo-coffin, ready to continue my serene passage through the stars. When I next open my eyes, I'll be looking out onto McQueen's World — *my* world — ready for a life that's everything poor dead Scarlett Hood ever dreamed of.

Jude Reid lives in Glasgow, Scotland and writes dark stories in the narrow gaps between her work as a surgeon, raising her kids and trying to wear out a border collie. Co-creator of the podcast audiodrama *Tales From The Aletheian Society*, and a contributing writer to the story-running fitness app *Zombies, Run!*, Jude has had short speculative fiction published in numerous anthologies and magazines. She's an active member of the Horror Writers Association, and drinks far too much coffee.

THE FAUN AND THE WOODCUTTER'S DAUGHTER • RUMPELSTILTSKIN • APPALACHIAN FOLK TALE

THE FOREST MAGIC PROTECTS ITS OWN

JAMIE LACKEY

Barbie grew up clear back in the holler, tucked right up against the base of the mountain. She spent her waking hours wandering through the woods, keeping her old pa company as he picked out the very best trees to cut and carve. He crafted the best furniture for three states around, and all sorts would come and request a piece, made special.

One early spring morn, when she was about eight years old, Barbie wandered off, following a trail of snowdrops bowing their heads in the gentle breeze. She figured she'd pick a handful and weave a crown for her stepmother, who stayed in, keeping house, too busy to come out and pick flowers for her own self.

But Barbie ended up wandering too far and got herself plum tuckered out. She plonked down on a mossy stone and tucked into her lunch, a cold ham sandwich on crusty bread. She scattered the crumbs for the birds and kept right still, so the birds and even a few squirrels scampered up and helped themselves to the feast.

Unbeknownst to her, another creature was watching from behind the trunk of a great tree. It was a young faun, who kept to himself so deep in the woods that he'd never spied a human afore, and he found himself mighty curious about the pretty little girl. The birds and squirrels didn't seem afeared, and he reckoned he was at least as brave as them, so he approached, his hooved feet silent on the soft ground.

Barbie looked up and saw him, standing in a slanted ray of sunshine. He looked to be about her age, with dappled skin and big brown eyes with long, dark lashes. There were two nubs sticking out of his tousled curls, just like the ones she'd seen on little baby goats. And his legs were like a goat's, too, furry and ending with two dainty cloven hooves.

"Oh, hello," Barbie said.

The faun had never spoken before, but there didn't seem to be much of a trick to it, and he figured it out pretty quick. "Hello. Who are you?"

"I'm Barbie. What's your name?"

"I don't have a name."

"How sad! Do you want one?"

The faun had never felt the lack of a name before, but suddenly he quite sorely wanted one, so he nodded.

"Well, then, I'll give you one!" Barbie tapped one finger against her lips, thinking. "How about Sebastian? I'll call you Bastian."

Bastian felt the name settle on him, felt it seep into him like rain on parched earth. "I like it," he said. "Thank you."

"Do you know any games?" Barbie asked.

They stacked rocks and threw sticks till dinnertime, when Barbie's stomach rumbled. "Oh, I should get home! My parents will be worried!"

Bastian hadn't a clue what a parent was, and wasn't happy to see his new friend go. But he also couldn't make her stay, if she wished to leave. He pressed a perfectly rounded stone into her hand. "This is for you, to thank you for my name."

As Barbie left the woods, her memory of the day evaporated like a puddle in the sun. She knew it had been a good day, that she'd been happy about something important. But she just couldn't recall what that had been.

He stepmother was cross that she was late for dinner, but pleased by the flower crown, even if it was a bit wilted.

Barbie kept the smooth stone in her pocket. It still made her happy, even if she couldn't recall why.

•

Years rolled by, like they do, and Barbie grew into a lovely young lady, the darling of the whole county. Sometimes, she'd still steal away to the woods. Bastian would meet her there, and they'd run and play or sit and talk, but the memory of him always faded the moment they parted. She kept his stone in her pocket, till the weight of it felt so familiar that it was like a part of her.

Sometimes she'd wrap her fingers around it and remember that there was something she'd forgotten.

"Why do I always forget you when we part, only to remember when I see you again?" Barbie asked.

"It is the magic of the woods," Bastian said. "It protects us from folk who would hunt us, would hurt us."

"I would never hurt you," Barbie said.

Bastian reached out and twined his fingers through hers. "Maybe not. But the magic doesn't know that. It only knows that you don't belong to it."

"I wish I did."

Bastian squeezed her hand. "Me too."

•

Times grew harder as the years passed, and Barbie's pa had fewer and fewer folks seeking him out. Why pay for a hand-crafted oak table when factory-made particle board would hold food off the floor just as well? But times weren't rough for everyone, and one day, a rich young man rolled into town. He kept his hair slicked back and wore a neat gray suit with a purple pocket square. He smiled like a fox, and Barbie suspected that he was both clever and cruel.

The rich young man gave his name as Mr. Jones, and bragged that his father owned a furniture factory.

He saw Barbie on his third day in town, when she was down doing the shopping for her stepmother. She was gazing at a poke of sweets with longing in her eyes, but not enough money in her pocket.

Her hair shone like burnished gold in the sun, and everything about her was all wholesome and sweet. Mr. Jones considered her for a moment, and decided that he wanted her for his very own.

He reached over her shoulder, plucked up the sweets, and paid for them like it was nothing. He tossed one into his mouth, and held another out to Barbie, smiling his fox-smile. "Would you like a candy?"

Barbie smiled back, just to be polite, but stepped away. "Oh, I couldn't. But I thank you for offering, Mr. Jones."

She hurried off without introducing herself. But of course, everyone in town was happy to tell him about her. Their kind, sweet girl. Fond of the woods, devoted to her parents. Poor as a church mouse.

He followed her into the woods the next day. She picked blackberries and hummed to herself, and every once in a while, she looked up like she was expecting someone.

The gossips hadn't mentioned anyone special, so Mr. Jones fancied that she was waiting for him. He walked right up to her, spinning a gold coin across his knuckles so it glinted in the sun. "I hear your father can craft tables worth their weight in gold," he said, throwing the coin in the air and catching it. "My father owns a furniture factory, you know. I know something about the value of a table, and I bet that such a feat is impossible."

"I don't hold with gambling, Mr. Jones," Barbie said.

"It sounds like you don't have any faith in your father's skills."

"My father is the best craftsman for at least three states around."

"Then why not take my bet? If he's as skilled as you say, you can't lose."

"And what do I get if I win?"

"Enough money that you can buy all the sweets you want, and never be hungry again."

"And what do you want if I lose?"

"Your hand in marriage."

Barbie gaped at him. "You don't even know me, Mr. Jones."

"I know value when I see it," he said. "I'll let you think about it."

After he was gone, Bastian came and found her crying. He stroked her hair. "What's wrong?"

"I'm trapped," she said. "When I tell my parents about Mr. Jones's bet, they'll want to take it. Because to them, we win either way. And I won't remember why I don't want to marry him. I won't remember you."

"Marrying him might be for the best," Bastian said. "He can take care of you, take care of your family."

Barbie shook her head. "I don't need some rich fellow to take care of me. And I couldn't ever love him."

"Why not?" Bastian asked.

"Because I love you."

Bastian had loved her since that first day, when she gave him his name, and every day since. He'd never dared to hope that she might love him in return.

He pulled three hairs out of his own curls and braided them together and twisted them into a ring so fine that it was almost invisible. Then he slipped it onto the ring finger on her left hand. "I love you, too. And I'll help you, if I can. But if you call on the magic outside the bounds of the forest, if you remember it when you shouldn't, it'll claim you. You'd never be able to leave the woods again."

•••

Barbie emerged from the woods, remembering only Mr. Jones and his bet. She told her parents of it with a heavy heart.

Her stepmother took her hands and twirled her around. "A right peculiar proposal, but a happy one!"

"Pa, you'll win, won't you?" Barbie asked.

Her father, seeing the fear on her face and the joy on his wife's, could only nod. "I reckon I can give it my best shot."

•••

Barbie forgot all about Bastian's promise, but the faun set right out to fix the contest. He begged dryads and nymphs and sprites for their assistance, and they guided Barbie's oblivious father to the perfect tree. He chopped it down and set to carving. It took three long days, but when he finished it was the finest work he'd ever done.

Mr. Jones brought a man in from his father's factory to evaluate the table. He was tall and thin, his face pinched and squinting. Barbie stood, squeezing her lucky stone tight in her hand, while this stranger held her future in his.

The price he eventually named was a little on the low side of fair. Mr. Jones grinned, sure he'd won. "Now, let's just get it weighed, and compare the weight to the value."

But when the gathered men went to lift it, it was like the wood was made of feathers. It hardly tipped the scale at all. "Well, it looks like it is worth more than its weight in gold after all," Barbie said, hardly able to contain her relief.

Barbie's stepmother happily claimed the prize money, chortling as she counted it.

Mr. Jones dropped to one knee, staring at Barbie as if she'd hung the moon. "You tricked me," he said. But he didn't seem vexed by his loss. In fact, he seemed proper pleased. "You are the perfect woman, I'm sure. Marry me." His tone made it clear it was more of a command than a request.

Barbie stared in horror. She'd expected him to give up, not dig in. He pulled a golden ring out of his pocket, grabbed her by the hand, and tried to slide it onto her finger.

But there was a ring there already.

"What's this?" he asked, turning her hand so the impossibly thin band caught the light.

"Bastian," Barbie said, remembering everything. It was his magic that saved her, his clever mind that had caught on the perfect solution. "Bastian!"

He appeared, looking strange and out of place outside the bounds of the woods. He held his hand out to her.

If she took his hand, she'd belong to the magic. Her parents would forget her.

But if she didn't take his hand, she was sure she'd never see Bastian again.

"I can't marry you, Mr. Jones," Barbie said. "Because my heart belongs to this here faun." She turned to her parents. She pressed her lucky stone into her father's hand. "You use that money to take care of yourselves, you hear?" Then she took Bastian's hand, and they ran back to the woods together, laughing and joyous.

Mr. Jones blinked and shook his head. He couldn't rightly remember what had just happened. There'd been a girl, with hair as gold as sunlight. But he couldn't quite recall her face. He shrugged and took himself right back out of town, since there wasn't anything worth sticking around for.

But his factory man stayed to talk to Barbie's pa. The factory was looking for folks what could design things, and he recognized talent when he spotted it.

And as for Barbie and Bastian, well, they was as happy as they could be, together in the woods. They faded right out of everyone's memory. The forest magic protects its own, after all. But Barbie's pa kept her lucky stone in his pocket, and sometimes, he and his wife would vanish into the woods for a few hours. They'd each return with a pair of flower crowns and no memory as of why.

Jamie Lackey lives in Pittsburgh with her husband and their cat. She has had over 160 short stories published in places like *Beneath Ceaseless Skies*, *Apex Magazine*, and *Escape Pod*. Her debut novel, *Left-Hand Gods*, is available from Hadley Rille Books, and she has two short story collections published by Air and Nothingness Press: *The Blood of Four Gods* and *A Metal Box Floating Between Stars*, and, most recently, the novella *The Forest God*. Jamie has contributed to *Cities of Dust*, *Planes of Light*, *Polis*, *NevermorEarth*, *NeverisEarth*, and the *NeverwasEarth* anthologies. In addition to writing, she spends her time reading, playing tabletop RPGs, baking, and hiking. You can find her online at jamielackey.com.

SCHNEEWITTCHEN · THE SELKIE BRIDE · FANTASY ·

WHERE THE EARTH MEETS THE SEA AND THE SEA MEETS THE SKY

BRENT BALDWIN

In the end, Bash swept up the wilted rose petals and made the eight beds a final time. He stacked the dishes and emptied the ice box. A perfectly fine cottage and no longer home to anyone.

He walked north, alone, until the forest gave way to the mountains and the mountains gave way to the sea. There, at the edge of a shingle beach stood another cottage. The thatch had slipped, and one shutter hung crookedly, but it would do. For a while.

He set his pack on the table and lit a fire in the hearth. The cottage soon smelled of well-traveled tea and honey. Over the following days he repaired and he tidied and he sat and he thought. The thoughts meandered from poison apples to iron slippers to wedding vows. He shook his head, putting the past aside, which was where he was when he saw her.

She walked down the shingle as if she owned it, though he couldn't imagine why anyone would want to own a heap of stones that existed only to defy the wind and the tide. She reminded him of the past, but her hair was the red of a well-stoked forge rather than the black of a forest at midnight. The sea behind her rolled with white-flecked waves that never seemed to reach her bare feet. When she saw him, her eyes narrowed.

She approached slowly and at an angle, as one might a dangerous animal. "You live here?"

Bash looked away, as was his nature, but the etiquette lessons from his past life took hold, and he returned his gaze to her and smiled a tentative smile. "For now. Might you like tea?" he offered. "Or scones?"

"What are scones?" she asked.

"Bread with honey and cream. You don't have to..."

"Perhaps just one," she said.

In the cottage, he pulled out one of the two kitchen chairs and offered it to her, then set the kettle to boil and fetched the scones from the basket beside the hearth. Oh, how he loved scones with warm honey.

"'s good," she said, around a mouthful of crumbs, and took another.

They ate and they drank and they listened to the crash of the surf and the crackle of the fire.

●●

Celia picked at the crumbs she had spilled. The fisherman would barely look at her, which would have been queer enough, but it was the way he moved that surprised her. The steadiness, as if he knew every cranny and current of the world and his place within it. Fishermen she knew, but none like this.

"I must be going," she said.

He brushed driftwood-brown hair from his eyes. "Safe travels, then."

On the beach, she stretched her legs and pressed into the wind. The salt spray tugged at her dress, threatening to spill her on the slick stones for the fisherman's amusement. She followed the spit of land as it wrapped around the bay. The sun dipped toward the horizon. She would need to go soon. It wouldn't due to be stranded. Again.

She crossed over the spine of the hills and back to the beach below the cottage. There, beside a crook in the boulders, her heart stopped.

It was gone.

Her heart restarted, but the blood it pumped had turned colder than a winter's morning. Her hands trembled. He was like the rest. Honeyed tea and honeyed words, but another thief of women and lives.

She marched up the beach, unsure what she could do, but ready to find out.

The fisherman was in the little garden beside the cottage, working a brush over… Over her skin, she realized. She crept forward, one hand held to her mouth, the other twisted into a claw.

The fisherman glanced up and saw her. He blinked, and his mouth formed an O.

"Is this… Oh, I'm so sorry."

Her skin shone like a newborn's, glossy and black with a swirl of gray on the left hip. He held it up with both palms upward, as if making an offering.

She took it and pressed it to her chest.

The fisherman studied his shoes. "I should have known."

"Yes, you should have." She raced to the sea, flinging the dress behind her and slipping into the waves as the last hint of the sun flashed green on the horizon.

• •

Bash packed a fishing rod and some lunch. The bay made for good fishing, but he hiked past the breakwater to fish among the swells. The barking of seals mixed with the crash of the waves.

After the solitude of the forest, it was enough to drive a fellow mad. The fish, at least, did not seem to mind. He caught a fair dozen and crossed back to the bay, pausing to toss a few of the smaller bream to the seals. They applauded his generosity.

The days of summer slipped into autumn, and the sea grew too rough for fishing. He mended the blankets and tended the cottage's garden. Each day he baked scones, just in case.

• • •

On the seventh tide after the spring equinox, Celia returned to the shore near the cottage. Seals sunned themselves on the outward side of the stony crescent that shielded the fisherman's cottage from the worst of the sea. She hid among them and looked across the bay.

The fisherman worked on the cottage, hewing fresh timbers and rethatching the roof. He worked, whistling quietly, oblivious to her presence. The smell of bread wafted on the breeze, mingling with the bay's brine.

Memories floated past. Other fishermen, other times. Her mother would have told her to stay at sea, but her mother had long ago given up on her human half. Perhaps she was right, but something kept tugging Celia toward the shore.

She slipped out of her skin and put on a simple brown dress. The sun dried her as she strolled up the beach.

The fisherman worked at a table outside the cottage. Bits of sawdust flecked his clothes.

He didn't notice her approach. "Might there be tea and scones here?" she asked.

He jumped. "Hello again."

Celia curtsied.

"A moment." He turned back to his table and finished sawing the board. When it was neatly stacked, he hurried into the cottage and returned with a teapot and a basket of warm scones. He passed her a teacup and set the basket on the work table.

"How did you know I would come today?" she asked.

"I didn't."

She sipped her tea. As she set her cup down, it slipped from her fingers. She tried to catch it, but only succeeded in spilling tea on the table and sending the cup tumbling. It bounced thrice and fell, shattering on the stones as the fisherman tried and failed to catch it, too. A shard struck him in the hand, leaving a deep scratch.

Celia silently cursed her stupid, traitorous fingers. "I'm so sorry."

The fisherman pressed a napkin over the wound. "It happens."

"I'll be back in a moment." He slipped into the cottage.

It was all her fault, and she couldn't leave him to tend his wound alone, so she followed him inside. He collected a needle and thread and positioned the needle over the scratch, but his hand shook as he took aim at the scratch.

"Can I help?" she asked.

"Does your kind know how to sew?"

"This dress did not make itself." She could not—entirely—keep the indignation out of her tone.

He passed her the needle.

She stitched him quickly but efficiently and knotted the thread.

"It will hold," he declared.

The thread puckered his weathered flesh. It looked wrong, and it was her fault. She didn't belong on the land, and it was foolish for her to have come back. Her clumsiness had hurt him, and he had only ever been kind to her.

"I... I should go." She stepped back hastily, knocking into a chair but catching it before she could break something else.

"But you've only just arrived." He didn't meet her eyes, but his tone was plaintive.

Her wild half heard the sea's call and yearned to rush back to it. The human half ached to stay and to learn more of this strange man.

A temporary truce, she decided, would not be out of order. "Do you have more scones?"

He chuckled with relief, and it warmed her more than the summer sun. "I can make them, if you'll grant me the time."

He whistled as he worked, a tune that felt familiar, but she couldn't place. The men of the sea sang so many tunes and told so many lies, they all turned into a blur over time. The fisherman was not of the sea, though, she knew that much. He had come from afar, and he would leave again. The kind ones always did. They might share a month or a season or a year, but they always had someone, somewhere waiting for their return.

The shadows grew as the sun descended, and by then her stomach was pleasantly stuffed with warm bread. She rose and curtsied. "I must go."

"I wish you wouldn't."

"I would stay for a time," she admitted, "but if I do not go soon, I will be trapped."

"When might I see you again?"

She considered the question. She could return in a few days, but perhaps better to wait and see if his interest waned. Or if her own did. "The seventh tide after the new moon."

"A propitious number." He rose and escorted her out of the cottage.

She took his hand and pressed it to her lips. Then she turned and fled, racing to the sea before the moon could fully rise.

The first hint of dawn had not reached the horizon, but Bash was awake and wearing grooves in the cottage floor with his pacing. He ought to move on, find his people again. Find a nice woman with a thick beard and a stout bed. The last thing he needed to be doing was—

The scones were burning.

He pulled them from the oven and set them beside it to cool.

By midmorning, she hadn't come. The seals gamboled around the breakwater, but if she were among them, he couldn't tell. The scones were covered, and even the tea had cooled.

If he spent the afternoon packing, he could be on the trail by nightfall. A long springtime hike would do him well after a damp winter.

He didn't see her approach, but when he looked up, she was there, a wry smile hung crooked on her face.

"What's that look?" she asked.

"Old memories." Bash sketched a bow. "I have tea and—"

"Scones?"

He motioned her inside. At the table, he passed her the scones and honey, but he also passed her a small jar. "You know jam?"

She slathered it on a scone and shoved the whole thing into her mouth. "It's amazing." Crumbs sprayed like breaking waves. She washed them down with a gulp of tea. "How did a man learn to make something so divine?"

"A… friend taught me."

She cocked her head. "Oh, do go on."

Bash looked away. What could he say? How could he explain living with six of his brothers in a house with a single woman? How could he explain the torment of her leaving, or the feeling of seeing her at the wedding, holding someone else's hand?

"One of those relationships, huh?"

"I suppose so," Bash said. "What about you? Does your kind…"

"Sometimes, if the goddess smiles upon us, our relationships don't even end poorly."

He didn't even have that much experience, only silent, foolish dreams. He counted the crumbs on the table.

"If I return," she took his hand, "will you be here?"

Life thrummed through him. Awareness of her, of himself. His journey back into the mountains could wait. "Yes."

She smiled, and her hand slipped from his. It was only when she had left that he realized she hadn't told him how long she would be gone. Not that it mattered.

• • •

Bash collected sand and reeds. He stocked plenty of wood and stoked a forge to craft two perfectly round glass disks. He whittled a frame and fashioned gum to the edges. The warmth of summer had given way to the chill of autumn by the time he finished, but the cold was like the embrace of an old friend. When he slipped into the water and submerged, a long reed gave him air from the surface and the glasses gave him a perfectly clear view of the harbor.

She met him inside the breakwater and swirled around him in a ballet of flippers and bubbles. Bash danced with her as best he could, but the steps were unfamiliar, and the reed did not support the exuberance he felt.

Celia changed into her dress and marveled that the fisherman gave her the space to do it, even though he surely ached to have her in his arms as much as she ached to be in them. She crossed the beach to the cottage. The first beams of dawn lit the basket of scones waiting on the table. Their scent filled the air. The fisherman stood beside the table and bowed.

"Don't be silly," Celia said, and threw herself into his arms.

He kissed her, and when he tried to pull away, she wrapped a hand through his beard and held him in place. His lips were as warm and soft as a summer's breeze.

The sun reached its zenith, but no one was outside to witness it. Later, satiated, they strode out to the shingle. She carried a basket and he carried a blanket. They climbed the hill behind the cottage and ate scones with honey and jam and looked out upon the sea, blue and glistening.

They made a life of compromises, and while not all were tea and scones, most were more than satisfactory. And there, where the earth met the sea and the sea met the sky, a dwarf and a selkie lived happily ever after.

Brent Baldwin is originally from the tree-swept hills of the Missouri Ozarks. He now lives in London with his wife, two daughters, and terrifying guard cat. If you find him without his hands on a keyboard or his nose in a book, it will probably be in the kitchen. His work has previously appeared in *Fireside Fiction*, *Flash Fiction Online*, and Flame Tree Press, among others.

COLOPHON

TYPEFACE:
CENTAUR MT

AAN20.05.2